Sebastian Grubb was born in Birmingham, UK, in August 1982 and still resides there. He attended Old Swinford Hospital School and Solihull Sixth Form College and has recently completed an IT-related course with the Open University. He has written and uploaded numerous short stories over the years; however, *Halia Rises* is his first published novel.

This book is dedicated to my late grandmother, Kate Davies.
She would have been proud to see this novel on the shelves.

Sebastian Grubb

HALIA RISES

AUSTIN MACAULEY PUBLISHERS
LONDON · CAMBRIDGE · NEW YORK · SHARJAH

Copyright © Sebastian Grubb 2025

The right of Sebastian Grubb to be identified as author of this work has been asserted by the author in accordance with sections 77 and 78 of the Copyright, Designs and Patents Act 1988.

All rights reserved. No part of this publication may be reproduced, stored in a retrieval system, or transmitted in any form or by any means, electronic, mechanical, photocopying, recording, or otherwise, without the prior permission of the publishers.

Any person who commits any unauthorised act in relation to this publication may be liable to criminal prosecution and civil claims for damages.

This is a work of fiction. Names, characters, businesses, places, events, locales, and incidents are either the products of the author's imagination or used in a fictitious manner. Any resemblance to actual persons, living or dead, or actual events is purely coincidental.

A CIP catalogue record for this title is available from the British Library.

ISBN 9781035890125 (Paperback)
ISBN 9781035890132 (ePub e-book)

www.austinmacauley.com

First Published 2025
Austin Macauley Publishers Ltd®
1 Canada Square
Canary Wharf
London
E14 5AA

I would like to wholeheartedly thank Austin Macauley Publishers for taking the time to read through my story and deem it worthy of publication. Also, for their tireless hard work and support in finally getting *Halia Rises* out in the public domain.

It was as I was berating a young recruit to the castle guard, a then ill-tempered and somewhat headstrong youth named Simon Fester, that I first noticed the odd discolouration to the sky. I had, of course, seen all manner of different skies over my 45 years in this land, from angry dark clouds looking ready to shower the earth with a never-ending cascade of water, to the beautiful golden sunset. However, this colouration was neither beautiful nor angry. It was just truly unusual.

I remarked upon it slightly later that day, once my training duties were done, to my old friend Brother Abel, who had been working steadily and tirelessly as the castle medic for no less than 40 long years at this stage.

"Oh, with all the livestock carcasses that need to be piled up and set aflame, I would imagine the combinations of putrid fumes soaring to the heavens would be enough to turn the very sky a nasty shade. I wouldn't worry, young Marcus; hopefully, once the farmers can figure out the cause of this pestilence, things will start to return to normal."

I appreciated Brother Abel's explanation; only I got the feeling of unease that he didn't truly believe what he was saying. For several weeks now, the livestock around our part of fair Halia had been largely stricken with a most hideous disease which resulted in death within 3 days of apparent contraction. The disease as yet had no name, and no farmers, herders, shepherds, veterinary experts, crop-growers, merchants or anyone else even remotely involved in the trading of farm produce had seen anything of the like.

With no apparent explanation for the disease, and thus no useful remedy, the farmer had little choice but to pile up their deceased herd and put them to the torch. Not only was this a horrible sight to behold for anyone present in the region, be they travelling folk or locals, but more seriously the burning heaps unleashed the most offensive stench, which could carry for miles in every direction. This stench would not only assault the nostrils, it could also make the eyes water, and in the cases of less constituted folk, could even invoke feelings of nausea. Plainly speaking, it was all becoming unbearable and the situation simply could not drag on indefinitely. An explanation at least was being demanded by more and more people.

Somewhat fortuitously for me, I was stationed and accommodated in the primary stronghold of the area, Carnagon Castle, which had wisely been built on a bluff of rock, commanding a dominant view of the region. Due to its exact location, we in the castle were spared the worst of the stench, unless the wind did not work in our favour!

Carnagon Castle had been my mainstay home for the past 10 years. During my employment at the castle, I had been responsible for overseeing the recruitment, training and equipping of the household guard. An arduous task no doubt, but ultimately rewarding as I saw those once scruffy and slouching recruits become men, resplendent in their full armour on St Regal's day each year, when the new appointments were awarded in the courtyard at Gutvast

Palace, the ancestral home of the Harbrandt dynasty. The newly declared household guard would stand to attention as Vincent Harbrandt himself would pace slowly down the line, inspecting each recruit with his steely eyes and often sharing a joke or two.

I had known Vincent Harbrandt for well over 20 years and considered him a friend. He was ultimately a good man who loved Halia. He was engaging, charming, gracious, reliable; however, like all of us, he had his weaknesses. He could be overly ambitious, and it had happened before that this ambition, some may even call it greed, had caused him to be misled and do things he later regretted. Unfortunately, I was not quite so friendly with Vincent's slightly older sister, Elaine.

Elaine was able to act charming on the surface and play the part at lavish parties, meetings, tournaments and even within the bedchamber. She could put on whatever façade the situation demanded and adjust her emotions and reactions accordingly. However, one never knew her true motives. I always saw her as something of a snake, a view I was never foolish enough to share with anyone else. Elaine's ears appeared to be everywhere, to the degree that even a quiet murmur to a friend in a cosy tavern could cost the murmurer his tongue, or if the murmur was especially seditious, his very life. It was clear to those 'in the know' that Elaine was able to control and manipulate her younger brother. Elaine was envious that the true control of the dynasty would never be hers, but she made damn sure that she would be the one making the decisions, even if her words had to come via her brother's mouth.

I am almost certain it was Elaine's nefarious doings that had opened the floodgates, swamping Halia with misery, panic and death. She made a deal with an outside entity she couldn't possibly understand or even hope to control.

The chaos began with a party that had been arranged one dark night at Carnagon Castle. The party was to be held in the main hall of the keep, which was spacious enough to accommodate hundreds of people. All day, servants, cleaners, carpenters, painters and assorted staff had been preparing the hall and the castle in general for the evening's celebrations. Boards were swept and scrubbed with cleaning solutions, walls were repainted in a brilliant white, cobwebs were removed, paintings and tapestries were brought out of storage before being cleaned and hung on the walls, fine oak tables were moved into the hall, fine silverware was polished. Essentially, no expense was spared and no effort was too much.

The finest impression had to be made for the party's most important guest, one Lord Va'heash. At the time of the party, I had very little idea of who or what Lord Va'heash was, as I was not in the habit of being consulted about diplomatic issues. I was ultimately still a soldier and followed orders from the higher lords. Despite my fairly senior rank in the castle, I was kept abreast of events on a need-to-know basis, and it seemed that on this occasion, I did not need to know the precise reasons for the party going ahead.

Later events and investigations would uncover what a terrible mistake the Harbrandts had made in dealing with a being such as Va'heash; however, at the time I was in the dark as much as basically everyone else. I was merely told that the castle was entertaining a visiting dignitary for discussions about a future partnership.

The first guests began arriving shortly after nightfall. It was not just the Va'heash element that had been invited, but numerous high-standing members of the aristocracy were also expected to attend. The nobles typically arrived in groups of three to four, usually a lord and lady accompanied by one or two personal staff. Warm greetings and pleasantries were exchanged and the fancy wine soon began to flow. Regional politics appeared to be the main topic of conversation; local culture, the current state of business and even some frivolous gossip could also be heard as I moved about the room, ensuring that everything was in order.

The subject of the burning livestock and hideous smell though was never going to be ignored. It was one Sir Flagg who first broke open that door of conversation. I assured him that I was as much in the dark as everyone else regarding the cause of the terrible plague. Sir Flagg voiced his concern that should the disease spread to humans, the land would be in for a very rough time. I shared his concerns, as would any sane person. Sir Flagg and I were on the topic of the construction of the new chapel in our capital city of Farchester, when a hush seemed to take hold of the room.

Conversation seemed to have stilled all too suddenly, although looking about the room, I could not ascertain what had provoked this change of tone. It was only later on that it made sense. We were all feeling much the same thing. In my case, it was a deep sense of unease, as if someone or something bad was approaching and relaxing was the last thing I needed to do. For others, I believe, that moment inspired nothing less than cold dread.

"The Va'heash party has arrived," a sentry could be heard proclaiming from the open castle door. I immediately made my way to the castle entryway; as one of the more senior soldiers on duty that night, I was expected to make a good impression and was in charge of most of the household guard for the duration of the party. I stood shoulder to shoulder with the sentry, almost subconsciously, as if we were expecting an attack. I could make out a group of figures climbing the slope through the darkness. At this stage, I could make out few details, only that the lead figure walked slightly ahead of the rest of the group, and also that one of the group seemed abnormally tall and broad of person. By this stage, Vincent and Elaine Harbrandt were also standing in the entryway, ready to greet their very important guest and offer a very warm welcome, a very foolish welcome, it would later prove.

Lord Va'heash finally walked into the circle of light thrown out by the burning sconces fixed to the exterior of the castle entryway. He stopped and offered what was intended as a warm smile; however, it was uncomfortable and unnatural and no way reached his unsettling pale eyes.

"My Lord Va'heash, we welcome you to Halia and to Carnagon Castle. You grace us with your presence. May I introduce you to my brother, Lord Vincent Harbrandt, Keeper of the Lafroide Valley?"

Lord Va'heash fixed Vincent with a glare, which lasted too long for comfort. I could feel Vincent's unease even from several feet away. Finally, Va'heash spoke, though with no real warmth or friendliness, "A pleasure, I'm sure."

This rather curt response seemed to put the Harbrandts on a slight back-foot. It seemed an inappropriate manner in which to greet a senior noble. However, I was not too judgmental in that moment, as I had travelled over my years and tried to be open-minded about the culture differences between various peoples.

"Please, c-come in-inside," stammered Elaine.

This reaction drew sudden glances from everyone present. Elaine was very much a public speaker, a strong diplomat, almost always seeming fearless and never afraid to show her claws if need be. She had shouted down and stared down numerous bishops, nobles and even high-ranking military officials over the years. However, in that instant, her defences were down, her armour lacking, any airs and graces swept aside. She knew that she was no longer in control of whatever might happen that night. If Elaine herself was not in control, then Va'heash was. I believe that many of us knew it then and there.

Va'heash accepted the welcome and followed the Harbrandts inside the castle, shortly followed by his retinue, all of whom went totally unintroduced and offered no greeting. They merely walked by, stone-faced and staring forward. The large man I had noticed earlier came fully into view, and I felt deep unease as he walked past me. I am no less than 6 foot 3 inches in height, and this brute TOWERED above me by a solid foot, if not more. He was also very broad in the shoulder and possessed arms thicker than many people's waists.

He, as well as the rest of Va'heash's retinue, was not dressed in any real finery, but had donned thick leather jerkins with padded trousers and solid boots. It was as if they wanted to appear smart, but also prepared, although they were all bare-headed and wore no real battle armour. The retinue was all powerfully built men, several with visible scars and what appeared to be tribal markings. They had the eyes of killers and possessed a general air of menace. It was clear to all that they were not diplomats, but no one dared ask exactly why they were there.

The large brute had stopped around a foot ahead of me and turned his huge brick of a head to look at me, or look DOWN at me, I should say. I knew that I should have returned his stare and held it, it was part of my job. But forgive me, I could not hold his stare and let him triumph in that small test. I felt an unease I had never felt before looking into those dark pits. I saw something inhuman there, something bestial, and had to look away all too soon. Other members of our castle staff witnessed this interaction, which shamed me even more. I was supposed to be the grizzled veteran and fearless one, who led by example. I felt small in that moment, small and weak.

Luckily, the brute continued after his master, but not without issuing a wicked chuckle at his triumph over me. Once the Va'heash retinue had all entered the great hall, I took up place at the rear of the party, leaving the sentries to continue standing watch.

Whilst we had been 'greeting' the Va'heash party, I could not help but notice that there was little sound coming from the great hall. The guests and staff had clearly not dropped their guard and were waiting for whatever was causing the anxiety to appear. Their wait was at least over, it seemed.

"My lords, ladies and fellow citizens of fair Halia, may I present Lord Va'heash, a dignitary from North Utresh? He has been invited in the hope that our two realms may broker an agreement and work to our mutual benefit."

Lady Elaine Harbrandt had clearly recovered some of her nerves after her initial shock; however, she still sounded off-beat and unconvincing in her introduction. She began the round of applause; I noted that the guests' response was as unconvincing as her introduction. Several guests present took up the clap, but I noticed that no one was smiling and the applause was less than what should be extended to a visiting dignitary. It could even have been called feeble, if not insulting. The party was off to a bad start, but I had no idea how much worse it would get even then.

Whilst I was making my rounds during the party, checking with my soldiers to see that all was well, and exchanging the odd word with a well-dressed guest, the place name of 'North Utresh' suddenly struck a bell. I had heard that name before, during a campfire tale long ago in my youth. The teller had been an old veteran who had lost a hand in battle and walked with a pronounced limp. However, despite his physical injuries, it was ultimately his experience which had caused the deepest scars, a hurt which never went away, he told us. The veteran, whose name I cannot recall, had travelled far and wide during his years in service of the army of Halia. He had visited dark and brutal lands over the years, but he was certain that the worst by far was Utresh.

The veteran would only recount some of his ghoulish tales from there. We, being young and foolish, tried to coax him into telling us more, but he became emotional, shook his head and left the fireside to be by himself. An uncomfortable quiet descended on the company, who had only moments before been a raucous and jolly company signing into the night. We never pressed the issue again; maybe some stories are just better off not being told.

Then, standing in that main hall, I had a nasty feeling that I would very soon discover first-hand how bad the Utreshians could be and I would no longer have to wonder about what that poor old veteran had been through.

Roughly one hour after the party had started, I approached the young recruit, Simon Fester, to ask him how his rounds were going and if he had anything he felt I needed to be aware of. By this stage, the guests had mellowed slightly and were speaking in smallish groups. About ten minutes prior to this, I had glanced over towards the dais and could clearly see Lord Va'heash engaged in conversation with Elaine Harbrandt. Although from my brief glance, it seemed clear that Elaine was doing most of the talking and Va'heash was content to sit and listen. Vincent himself stood nearby, speaking to an elderly noble dressed in an embroidered purple robe. I had exchanged a brief nod and smile with Vincent, who appeared to be enjoying the evening for what it was worth.

Simon paused momentarily and a cautious look crossed his face, immediately giving me the suspicion that he did have something he wished to tell me.

"No real problems, sir, it's just that, I seen three of them big folk who came with Lord Va'heash head off down that corridor, alone, only a few minutes back. It may be nothing, they may just be looking for the privy. Just letting you know," Simon responded.

I thanked Simon for his information and advised that I would personally check up on this situation. Simon had indicated a corridor that went towards several possible locations—the main kitchen, the larder, the buttery, the storeroom, the brewery, and the cellar entrance. I made my way in that direction keeping an eye out for the three retainers.

I reminded myself to remain cordial and helpful if I did see them and not come across as one issuing a challenge. I was not looking for any manner of confrontation.

I paused, and even held my breath without knowing, as I heard urgent sounding voices coming from down the corridor. The language was foreign to me and I could not make out a single word. The voices sounded bizarre though, overly deep and not a voice one would expect from human vocal chords. I became increasingly apprehensive about approaching this situation alone and wearing no real protection.

I had been advised to dress formally, which in castle code translated to no heavy armour. I was wearing my trusty longsword at my waist, the leather handle of which I now gripped almost instinctively. I knew I could not stand idly in the corridor, so almost on impulse I began creeping slowly towards the unusual voices. As I got closer, I was able to recognise that the sound was coming from the room housing the cellar entrance. Why would the three retainers be messing about with the entrance to the cellar?

In a moment, which seemed to last all too long, the horrific reality of the situation came crashing down. All sorts of alarms started sounding in my mind. I knew that I had no time to turn back and gather more men. The sound of a trapdoor slamming open and more voices becoming audible cemented my next action. I drew my longsword fully, before moving towards the cellar room at a full sprint, any subtlety now cast aside.

I rounded the corner not knowing exactly what awaited me, but knowing that it would be nothing pleasant and that polite words were already off the table. The sight was worse than I had expected, but at the same time, exactly what I had expected. The solid wooden trapdoor was wide open and a large man, of the same bearing and ilk as the other eight who had accompanied Va'heash, was in the process of ascending into the room, with half of his body on the stairs and half above the floor level. Another man, this one wearing heavier armour and brandishing a large ugly-looking cleaver, was already in the room with the original three retainers. My eyes met with theirs as I drew breathlessly into the doorway, and in that instant those five dark and murderous sets of eyes told me one thing—this was a kill or be killed situation.

Five on one. Five large and brutish-looking warriors, who were already producing 6-inch daggers, against one man with a longsword. Rushing in and trying to go toe-to-toe with them was suicide, so I adopted a defensive stance with my longsword and slowly edged back. Let them come to me, I thought; with the benefit of the doorway, I could perhaps fight them one-on-one.

However, they did not come to me. The man in the process of ascending the stairs came fully into the room, issuing a feral snarl at me. His teeth were yellow, somewhat fanged, and he also produced the same large ugly cleaver his comrade was holding. I saw another head appear at the top of the ladder and could hear the sound of more feet pounding up the cellar ladder. They were ignoring me, knowing I could not attack them presently, and quickly gathering what seemed to be an assault force into the castle proper. I did the only half-sensible thing I could do in that situation—I ran.

I made to run towards the main hall, where the bulk of the party was in progress. As if my state of panic was not enough, I could hear sounds of violent struggles coming from the direction of the hall. It seemed that there was some manner of coordination between the group in the cellar room and the remainder of the 'attendees' who had been prowling menacingly around the main hall. A multi-pronged attack was in progress. I entered the main hall at full sprint, and the situation was every bit as bad, if not worse, than the mental picture I had established during my short but frantic run down the corridor. At least seven of the household guard lay still and bloodied on the floor, with shocked and screaming guests being herded into one group at the far end of the hall. I noted that alongside the seven bloodied guards lay several well-dressed members of the nobility, their eyes blank and staring into nothingness. One had been decapitated fully, the head nowhere near the body. Whether they had attempted to foolishly wrestle with Va'heash's brutes and had paid the price, or simply been killed to make a point, I never knew.

I turned my head to witness an ongoing struggle, bold young Simon Fester desperately fending off a brute using his longsword. Whilst he was still green and had never been truly bloodied in battle, he had been progressing with his swordplay in the castle training ground and it was that practice and persistence which was most likely his primary reason for still standing. I could see that the brute would win this one unless I stepped in immediately. He was getting the upper hand in the duel by sheer strength and ferocity and driving Simon back towards the wall, despite only being armed with a 6-inch blade which had been concealed somewhere about their person. The brute's swings looked to be incredibly powerful and Simon's whole body was shaking with each block.

I dashed towards the duelling pair, and whilst I think it craven to attack a man from the rear, this situation spared no room for chivalry and genteel. I plunged my longsword deep through the man's leather jerkin and into his lower torso. I say 'plunged' but 'forced' would be a more accurate term, as it felt like driving the sword through solid clay. The brute's whole physical composition appeared to be different to that of a Halia man, or any other man I had encountered.

Whilst such a grievous wounding would have brought even a hardened battle veteran to his knees, the brute remained standing and his reaction was more of shock and anger than pain. He turned to see who had committed this gross insult to his person and fixed me with feral, beast-like eyes. Any vestige of humanity removed and cast aside now that their plan had come into play. The brute pressed a palm to the considerable wound to stem the bleeding, but still remained standing and his knife had not even dropped from his clenched and bloodied grip.

Whilst I was preparing for a follow-up strike, one that I hoped would put him down, a shining length of sword magically burst through the brute's right eye socket, to the tune of about 3 inches. Young Simon had taken advantage of my attack to organise his own. Simon was unable to wrench the sword from the brute's skull, so wisely let go of the blade as the brute finally slumped to the ground in a messy heap. Simon stood panting, eyes wide in fear and shock, whole body shaking with adrenaline. If I possessed doubts about the lad's courage, they were gone now.

"Well done, Simon," I spoke, nodding in appreciation.

"Well done, indeed, young Simon. The two of you managed to kill one of my soldiers, using backhanded attacks. How brave. Already you Halia *men*...are proving what you are really made of!"

I turned to see Lord Va'heash himself step forward, a grim smirk spread across his face. His comment had elicited a round of mocking laughter from the brutes, all of whom still stood. Some had been slashed and wounded by the household guard, but simply not enough, it seemed. These Utreshians could take quite a lot of damage, and gladly deal it out as well. I could hear the sound of screams and the clash of steel echoing throughout the larger castle. The Utreshians who had entered via the cellar entrance were already at work. I could only hope that some of the guards were making a defiant last stand and had managed to make a mark against these bastards before they went to whatever great beyond lies ahead of our all too short mortal lives.

These Utreshian brutes had managed to defeat the guards in the main hall with minimal armour and basic daggers, so it would make perfect sense that Utreshians wearing heavier armour and swinging large heavy blades would carve through the remaining guard like a sharp scythe through soft wheat.

The castle had been taken, it was a tough fact to face, but delusion benefits a man nothing. Va'heash was now in charge of the castle, and everyone in it, including me. I could not see either of the Harbrandts as my eyes quickly scanned the crowd. Unnervingly, Va'heash seemed to read my thoughts.

"Oh, your fine friends the Harbrandts are now MY guests, confined to their chambers under strict guard. I may have a use for them, or I may not. If not, I'm sure my hounds would love to feat on noble flesh."

This comment also drew a grizzly round of chuckles from the throats of Va'heash's kill squad.

"It seems I may need YOU, however, Marcus Kane. I was told by a little…someone…that you know this castle well, and the surrounding area, and about military strength. I may also have use for that knowledge, so it would be in YOUR interest to comply."

In that moment, I knew that I was beaten. I could not hope to escape or fight my way through all these deadly and ruthless killers. However, I could help another escape. I held my sword loosely at arm's length in a relaxed grip and walked forward slowly, as if to give myself up. The Utreshians appeared to be accepting the display, as none really made a move to intercept me. Va'heash himself appeared to be smiling, as if grateful that I was capitulating so meekly.

I suddenly switched the grip in my wrist so that my sword was ready to be swung. I had one swing and one swing only to get the job done. I swung hard and fast at the rope which was currently holding the heavy cloth in place high in the ceiling. Whether the Utreshians had been told of this feature or not, I never knew, but if they had then they may have taken a precaution to somehow disable it so that it could not be used against them.

To my joy, the rope was cleanly sliced and the heavy curtain swiftly dropped, a curtain which was used to partition part of the hall from the rest. The curtain had mainly been used over the years to hide the backstage goings-on during stage plays and enactments. I had never guessed it would be used for this purpose.

Even as the cloth was falling, I screamed for Simon to 'RUN' and I hoped that his initiative would kick in and he would know which door to take. For, in fact, it was not really a door at all, but a large painting which opened on hidden hinges to reveal a narrowish passage which led to the castle exterior via several winding passages. It was a secret known to a few in the castle, one that was guarded well. I had shared this secret with Simon earlier that evening, almost unconsciously, as if I didn't know quite why I was sharing this guarded information with a recruit. They say that the Gods work in mysterious ways, and maybe the Gods favoured Simon that night.

As soon as the heavy curtain hit the ground, my only goal was to buy Simon as much time as I could, as I was not sure if Simon would be able to fully close the painting entrance from the other side, and if not, it would be a quick and easy chase. I put one foot on the bottom of the curtain and started swinging for all I was worth. I would meet the Gods as a warrior who went down fighting for his land. What better way to go out?

I put my full force into each blow and bellowed a roar which came from deep within me. Despite my best efforts to intimidate the enemy, they moved forward all too fast. The brutes formed a semi-circle around me and closed in with weapons raised. Whilst they were obviously tough and capable, none seemed overly eager to get slashed with a sharp longsword, and that thought actually brought a chuckle to my lips.

The chuckle was halted all too soon when I felt a strong wrist grab my left elbow and drag me roughly to the ground, where the fight basically ended. I just had time to look up before a huge boulder of a fist came flying towards me. Then…nothing.

I found myself walking alone through the lands of Halia, but it was not the Halia I remembered. It seemed day but the sky was unnaturally dark; it was not just the ominous grey thunder clouds I had seen so often, but more a sickly yellowy green, as if the entire sky was diseased. The sight was so unsettling I had to lower my gaze and try and focus on the ground, only to find that the ground was not much more pleasant to behold. The few remaining crops were withered and rotting. Large, deformed rats scurried about in the fields looking for any sustenance they could sink their yellow fangs in to. There were emaciated animals mindlessly staggering around, not to mention corpses randomly strewn across the landscape. Carrion feasted happily on these corpses, whilst bloated and ugly-looking swarms of flies descended up dead and near-dead alike.

Any visible building appeared to have been plundered or partially destroyed, as if roaming bandits had been afoot in the region. Then there was the stench, which was so foul that it assaulted the eyes and mouth as well as the nose. It made the eyes water and was so overwhelming it could even be tasted on the rancid air.

I noticed a figure staggering towards me across the wasted land. He, like the rest of the scenery, appeared malnourished and wasted. As he came slightly closer, I could make out the desperate and haggard face of Vincent Harbrandt. His finery was long gone and there remained nothing regal or noble about his bearing. He wore only tattered trousers around his pale and bony legs and his feet were bare and filthy. Vincent spotted me, his eyes frantic and tearful. "What have I done, Marcus? What have I done!" Vincent shrieked in despair.

"Is this Halia, Vincent? Where are we? What happened?" I asked in desperation, as lost and confused as poor Vincent.

"Wake up, scum!" A loud and nasty voice seemed to boom from the sickly and dark heavens. "Wake up, scum!" The voice repeated at the bars of the cell door.

As I slowly re-emerged back into the land of the living, I realised that I had been dragged from one nightmare into another, as the events of the night started jumping back into my foggy brain. Lord Va'heash, the attackers coming through the cellar entrance, the nobles being held hostage, my frantic last stand against the Utreshians. Then, almost as an afterthought, my mind went to young Simon, and I hoped with all my heart that he had somehow managed to escape the castle. I knew I shouldn't ask, but I couldn't hold my tongue. My jailor was still within earshot after dumping my meagre plateful of food through the 3-inch slot under the door.

"The soldier I was with when the curtain fell down, what happened to him?" I enquired, hoping for the best but fearing the worst.

The jailor smirked, displaying two rows of large, almost wolf-like teeth. His eyes looked yellow and wicked in the dark of the corridor. It seemed that these Utreshians looked as bad as they acted. They were rotten through and through.

"Oh, that little runt! We found him and had some fun with him. We all had a go." The jailor laughed again as he saw the pain register in my eyes. "Oh yeah, we like them young and fresh. He's swinging in the courtyard with a load of the others who we didn't need anymore."

I turned my head away from the door and tried to control my breathing. I would not let this animal see my weakness. I clenched my jaw and bit back the tears. *Poor Simon*, I thought to myself. I had done what I could in the moment. *I'm so sorry, Simon.*

In those hours of darkness, I had time to think. Too much time, in all honesty. It was really all I could do in that dark and wretched cell. I put some pieces together during that time.

Elaine. I could not help but think that Elaine had let her ambition get the better of her and made some manner of deal with this Lord Va'heash, someone none of us even knew. She had most likely not consulted any of her advisors over this. I knew that Vincent had not been given much say in this supposed deal and that his sister had been the driving force. Exactly what deal she was making to strike, I did not know at the time. She clearly had not known, or even begun to comprehend, who she had been trying to bargain with.

I did not know what state the Harbrandts were in, how many of the guests still lived, how many of the household guard were still living, how many enemy troops were in the area, or how far they had advanced through the land, as I knew even from my fuddled state in a dark and deep cell that Va'heash was not going to stop at his annexation of Carnagon Castle. I knew that I could not lie here helplessly waiting to get tortured for information before meeting my maker in some gruesome way. I had to get out of this cell.

I paused and took several deep breaths. I focused on my present state with as much clarity as possible, blocking all else out—the past, the future, everything. I thought about the layout of the castle I had lived in for the past 10 years. How well did I really know it? How could one escape the castle? What exits did I have, regardless of how unpleasant they may be? The main entrance was absurdly out of the question and would be even if I was clad in plate armour with the largest sword I could find. No, my exit had to be as discreet as possible. Then, in my state of deep focus, an answer came to me. I found a glimmer of hope, but also shuddered at what I would have to go through, figuratively as well as literally.

The castle's sewer system was fairly primitive compared to the more modern and better-financed buildings of Halia, especially in the splendid capital of Farchester. The waste, be it from privies, kitchens, the slaughterhouse or washrooms, was all funnelled into one large pipe, which fed out of the castle exterior into a specially built ditch cut into the hillside. If I could somehow get myself into this main outlet tunnel, I would be expelled into the ditch.

One concern was that I had never studied the exact length of the drop. In all fairness, I had never fathomed that I would be placed in a situation where I would have to exit the castle in such an extreme fashion. What if I went headfirst through the tunnel and dashed my head on the rocks some 50 feet below? What if I broke a leg and lay moaning until some Utreshian came to finish me off? What if I got stuck in a pipe and drowned? So many terrible outcomes assaulted me and tried to break my resolve. But I knew that my resolve was all I had right then. Remaining in that cell was not an option.

I lifted my head to look around me and see what I had in the cell. I was clad only in my underclothes, obviously unarmed. Within the cell, there was the small basic cot on which I lay, a feeble-looking wooden chair, a basin with a little pool of rank-looking water within, and the small round metal plate that had been placed under the door, still bearing a meagre portion of unappetising food. I used my hands to scoop the food into my dry mouth, trying to ignore the bad taste and focusing on getting it inside me. I would need all the energy I could get and had no room to be fussy that the cuisine was not up to scratch! I also downed the rank water, as I did not know when I would next have access to even semi-drinkable water. Survival was my only goal right then, comfort be damned!

I looked down at what passed as a privy in my cell. It was simply a hole in the corner of the room. I knelt to get a closer inspection, already trying to get used to the odour as best I could, given that I knew this was mild compared to what I would have to face. It was presently too small to climb through for a man my size. I scraped my fingers around the opening, testing the quality of the plasterwork. I found it crumbled away quicker than I had expected and was somewhat powdery. Then, it came to me in the darkness. The damp! A conversation suddenly sprung to mind from somewhere buried. A conversation my mind had likely found irrelevant so just stored it away somewhere. At that moment though, it came back to me as anything BUT irrelevant.

I had been discussing the general state of the castle with one of our local stonemasons some four months previously—a seasoned and hardworking expert named McCliff. He had the tendency to go rambling on about all sorts of issues relating to stonework, building, construction, laying of plaster, bridges, archways. Some of it interesting but sadly much of it not. But there in the darkness, what he had said about the damp deep in the castle came back to me.

I began scraping away more eagerly around the rim of the hole, putting more drive behind my claw-like strokes in my eagerness to see if the dampness really was affecting the consistency of the plasterwork. I felt my spirits rise as more and more plaster came crumbling away from the edge of rim and plunged down into the murky darkness. I counted my blessings that the jailor had not taken the trouble to fully check the cell but just dumped me in there. There was hope!

The hole was currently around 1 foot in diameter, and I would need no less than 2 feet if I was to squeeze my body through, as I could not run the risk of my rather broad upper body becoming stuck. My mind turned over that horrible fate, trapped upside down with the blood rushing to my head, totally at the mercy of my Utreshian jailors. That was not an option.

After 30 minutes of scraping away at the maximum intensity that my tired hands would allow, I was nearing the 2-foot hole that I felt minimum for an exit. More would be preferable, but I knew that every second in that fetid place worked against me. I felt desperation build in those moments and become almost suffocating. I briefly paused in my frantic pursual of what I hoped would be my final few moments of digging, to listen more closely to what sounded like a door being slammed nearby.

I had not imagined the slam, for the sound that followed made perfect sense, the dual sounds of footsteps, which were all too hurried for my liking, and the metallic jangling of keys. Someone was coming, most likely directly towards this cell. I had been fed my daily rations already, so the jailor was coming for another purpose, one that would likely entail me being taken somewhere else. If that did happen, then there was nothing to stop the jailor from seeing the hole I had been enlarging and put two and two together. I knew little about the wisdom or mental prestige of the Utreshian people, although I doubted any would be THAT stupid.

Could I squeeze down that hole in its present state? I wished that I could, but ultimately knew that I couldn't; it was still too small. I needed just a little more time and knew then that I would have to make it for myself, no one would give it to me. I looked around the room for anything that could be used as a makeshift weapon, my years of combat experience giving me ideas that would not occur to a more peaceable person. In those fleeting moments, I went with the chair leg, which of course could be and indeed was obtained by smashing the feeble chair against the stone cell walls.

Clutching the chair leg, my one and only weapon in the world, I tried to control my ragged breathing and do what I could to slow my pounding heart. I put my back against the wall of the cell as close as I could, right by the door, and waited for the sound of the key to turn in the lock. My plan was to drive the spike of the chair leg as fast and hard as I could into the jailor's exposed eye socket. He had not worn any manner of face protection the last time I saw him and I prayed that this weakness had not been amended. Sadly, this precise plan was somewhat thwarted when, instead of the key being turned in the lock, I heard a different sound. One that only increased my terror.

"Show yourself, stand in the middle of your cell with your hands displayed," growled the not-so-foolish jailor.

So much for the chair leg to the eye. The jailor was clearly no dullard, and this was evidently not the first time a prisoner had attempted some manner of trickery in a bid to escape. I should have known it would never be that straightforward. As my head was turned in the general direction of the door, my eye noticed ANOTHER potential weakness—the keyhole. My chair leg may not be quite so redundant as I had thought. If I could ram the spike in far enough, then the lock would be jammed and the jailor would be denied the immediate entry he was hoping for.

I took a deep breath and stepped in for my strike, driving the spike in a curve as smoothly and accurately as my increasing desperation and terror would allow. Praise be, the spike actually stuck the first time and the end seemed to disappear into the lock, to the tune of about 1 inch. I got myself behind the chair and leg and drove further, with all my might, wriggling and coaxing, trying to get the broken wood in as far as possible. I was by now in full view of the jailor, but stealth or secrecy was no longer an option. I stepped back panting and sweating, looking at my handiwork and just hoping that it would buy me the last few minutes I needed. If it didn't then I would deal with whatever came next. I had no time to wonder if my life would be spared for a second time.

I heard the yelling of the jailor as I turned and dived towards the almost finished hole, my intended exit out of there. I tried to block out whatever he was saying. The jailor could see exactly what I was doing, but as long as he could not reach me for the next few moments, I had a fleeting chance. I glanced back occasionally during those last few minutes to check that the door was holding. The jailor alternated between banging furiously on the solid door and jiggling his key in the now blocked slot, neither of which gained him any advantage. I had heard him yell for assistance one or twice, but his comrades were out of earshot as no one attended him, either that or they felt that they were being summoned for some filthy task beneath them, like changing a prisoner's soiled clothes or forcing them to eat. I counted myself lucky in that moment for the general Utreshian lack of vigilance.

Finally, I judged that the hole in the cell floor was large enough for me to squeeze through. As I readied myself to jump feet-first into whatever foulness lay waiting down there, I turned my head one last time to check on the progress of the jailor. I did not see the jailor at the bars any longer; what I did see however made me almost freeze in terror and I was beyond any kind of relief that at least my escape route was ready. For the large, monstrous face of the giant I had seen earlier glared in at me with furious intensity. He, or it, grinned wickedly and held up the head of an enormous sledgehammer to the bars. The hammer itself must have been so large that only a beast like that could wield it. The giant proceeded to swing the hammer into the door lock with such frightening force that the whole castle seemed to shake. In fact, the whole world seemed to shake. I did not wait for a second strike. I sent a final prayer to the heavens and launched myself feet-first into that wretched and foul darkness beneath.

The next part of the story is something I hesitate to put down in words, even considering all the other horrific ordeals I endured during the Utreshian invasion. Needless to say, it was incredibly harsh on ALL my senses and required willpower and perseverance I am not sure I will ever be able to summon again. That first fall was my main concern, as I had never measured how deep that first latrine pit was, or how deep the filth would be. 'Luckily' for me, the fall was only about 10 feet, although in that oppressive darkness I felt like I was falling for minutes on end.

I landed with only a slight jar, in what felt like thigh-deep liquid. In those awful moments, my only real guidance was the sound of escaping refuse, as I had no concept of compass-point direction down there. Occasionally, the foul refuse was shallower and swilled nastily around my knees, other times I found that I had to almost paddle in it. My primary concern was not allowing the foul stench to render me unconscious, as such a response would have most likely earned me a very unvaliant death.

All the while, I was not only trying to prevent myself from being overcome by the assault on my nostrils, ears and skin, but also the knowledge that the Utreshians knew where I had gone and were likely trying to work out my most likely method of exit. I prayed that I would triumph in that aspect, as I would be all kinds of vulnerable as and when, or even IF, I escaped the castle proper.

It was when I noticed the gloomy area had become slightly lighter, that I knew my ears had not failed me and I was indeed progressing in the right direction. I cannot adequately express my relief when I finally came into view of the outflow pipe and could at least put this foul stench behind me. The pipe was narrowish and would require some shuffling, but praise be, it was wide enough. I wasted little time in adopting a prone position, stomach down, neck craned forward. I was unfortunately face-deep in filth in that position, but it could not be helped. I did my best to keep any of that muck from getting inside my mouth somehow.

I shuffled forward for 10 feet or so until my head was physically poking out of the pipe, and out of the thick castle walls. Luckily, this exit and potential entrance was not well-defended, as it was folly for any commander to try and get his forces within a castle via a small stinking tunnel which was basically a dead end anyway, and a dark and stinking one at that.

I moved my head around freely, scouting the immediate area in the darkness to see if I could detect light and movement with my eyes or hear telltale sounds with my ears.

I could not detect any real movement other than the gentle swaying of trees in the breeze and the odd bat out for a nightly adventure. However, from the corner of my vision, I could spot several faint glows of orange standing out in the void of blackness. They were coming from the direction of the castle entrance, and it did not take a sage to work out who they were or what they were searching for. I knew my time was short, and remaining in that tunnel was not an option. For all I knew, a bold and fearless Utreshian was right now paddling through the filth behind me, snarling and bloodthirsty, oblivious to the stomach-churning essence around him.

I looked directly down to see what the drop was like and took some comfort in the fact that the fall was not long enough to make injury likely. I could make the jump, even in my present state, but it had to be done quickly. I shifted more of my body out of the pipe until I was almost at the waist, half in and half out, the refuse slowly sliding past me to disappear into the darkness. I stole another look at where the orange beacons had been, and it was no real shock that they were getting bigger and closer. I could discern at least four torches, likely more; I did not have time to ponder the issue. I knew that when I did drop, it would need to be feet-first, as I had when hastily departing my cell. This meant that I would have to reverse my body position.

I achieved this by gripping the under ledge of the exit pipe with a firm grip and flipping my body forward, which I performed surprisingly easily. This left me dangling by my arms, facing outwards into the night, with thin dribbles of filth directly in front of my face. I closed my eyes, took another deep breath and released my grip.

I was not blindly dropping into nothingness, as whilst I had never studied the drop from outflow pipe to solid ground, I knew that I would be hitting a mud slope first after my brief period of free-fall. My subsequent landing felt rough in the darkness and my entire skeletal structure shook all too painfully, but my adrenaline likely blocked out most of the pain. I slid feet-first in the muck for a brief period, before I ran out of momentum and came to a full rest. I could see little in the dark but knew that I was surrounded by large objects that should not have been there. It was then that I took the option of lying perfectly still, arms splayed out, trying to appear as dead as possible, as the wash of torchlight lit up the area.

"Do you think he came this way?" a rough voice enquired, before being promptly answered by an agent who was apparently in immediate charge of the party.

"Hard to tell with all those shit-covered corpses piled up. I'm not about to go through them all. Valak, take three others and scout the area, search for a trail, take the hounds if you need to."

At least my curiosity about the large objects had been sated. Luckily, my head was turned away from the firelight, so I did not have to worry about betraying my living body with unwanted facial tics, or having to hide the look of raw fear I felt. I held my breath as much as I could, as I could not tell how closely the Utreshians were watching and whether a gently rising body would be noticed even amidst all those corpses.

Finally, the torchlight seemed to move away, as did the voices. Still, I could not see what was happening behind me; was one of those creatures standing quietly, waiting, knowing my ruse, tricking me into revealing myself? I did not know, but what I did know was that I could not lie here covered in filth, amongst these stinking corpses, for much longer. I did not know how far away dawn was and knew that I had to be away, somewhere, anywhere, before then. I had to clean myself, find water and sustenance, find some decent clothing, get a weapon, try and locate any survivors, maybe find someone who could put parts of the story together, and once that was all sorted, devise a response. A response that would most likely involve trying to fight back against this monstrous invasion and protect the Golden City of Farchester.

Right then, it all seemed like climbing a mountain, weak and tired as I was. An insurmountable task I could not hope to perform. Strangely though, deep in my mind, I found myself shooting back through the years until I was there on Redcrag Mountain, still a boy at 10 years old. My tall and strong father, who was something of an adventurer, had taken my older brother and I on our first serious mountain trek. I was back there in my mind, teeth gritted, driving my little legs up a steep slope, trying to ignore the pain that was pestering my whole body. I looked up into the wind and saw my father at the top of the slope. He seemed as tall as a giant, his large frame silhouetted against the bleak rainy sky. I recalled his booming words deep in my mind, "One foot in front of the other, Marcus. Rise, and don't look back."

Right then, in that dark and horrid corpse-strewn waste ditch, I heard those words again, loud, almost as if my father was standing there speaking to me. I could not help but jerk my head in the direction I thought they had come from but saw no one. *Time to move, Marcus, one foot in front of the other. Time to rise.*

I started heading south under the remaining cover of darkness. North, I was fairly certain, was where the Utreshians had come from, and with the regional bastion of Carnagon Castle fallen, there would certainly be more coming from the north to reinforce the minor force which had overrun the castle. They had not tried to take the castle though sheer assault, which may have damaged it beyond usefulness, so they were clearly treating it as some manner of base.

Thankfully, I came across a stream of fresh water, which ran through a small valley sprinkled with birch trees. The tall, unmoving sentries watched silently as I both slaked my thirst and washed the worst of the filth from my body. As I possessed no hunting tools, meat was likely off the menu, so I gathered whatever berries, leaves and forest offerings I could in a small, discarded sack I had appropriated after raiding an old farming hut, which had otherwise been empty.

In the process of scouting for sustenance, I could not help but notice that much of the vegetation was in a sickly state. I came across plants withered and brown and saw that some of the younger trees were shedding leaves way out of season, not to mention the stunted and deformed-looking fruit. It was in that moment that my feverish nightmare came back to me; I once again saw that desolate wasteland of a landscape in my mind's eye. The progress of dawn revealed more of that deeply worrying and sickly-looking cloud cover. Whatever it was, it now appeared deeper and more severe. There was a sun up there somewhere, but no strength of it was reaching the land. It appeared to be more of a bizarre 'half-night' than actual day. However, pondering over it served me no purpose and I could do nothing to change it, so I continued south.

Around half an hour of steady walking, for I had not the strength for an all-out march in my present state, brought me to the once pleasant village of Otter's Wall. However, any pleasantry seemed to have disappeared along with the sun, for it was clear that the chaos that had enveloped Carnagon had not stopped there. Many of the wooden dwelling doors lay wide open, as if flung wide in terrible haste. Piles of clothing, toys, loose food, bedding, tools and more lay strewn about in no order, as if residents had left in haste and not cared if anything less than vital was dropped. The smouldering remains of some small fires added their black smoke to the already diseased-looking sky. I proceeded further into the village, cautiously, for I was still both unarmoured and unarmed. I did carry a snapped-off branch as a last-resort weapon, but this was more for a feeling of security. I knew that I would fare poorly against a weapon of forged metal swung by the huge muscular arms of an Utreshian warrior.

It was then that I saw the first of the bodies, already attracting swarms of bloated-looking flies and other insects looking for sustenance. I could not hate them, they had to eat what they could, as I had been doing that night and morning. The nearest body was that of an elderly man, sprawled face-up, staring blankly into the yellow brown heavens. An inspection of the body revealed no wound or serious injury. I was standing totally still and looking down at what had until recently been a living breathing being, when a familiar voice interrupted my thoughts, "I think he died of pure fright."

I jerked instinctively and brandished my feeble stick in the direction of the voice, on edge and caught off-guard. However, even in that raw state, it was only a moment before I recognised the owner of the voice.

Kindly Brother Abel had taken a few steps back and was holding his arms out in front of him as if to ward off an evil spirit or a large angry dog. "It's me, Marcus, it's me, Brother Abel."

I relaxed and allowed myself a sigh of relief. Without another word or any hesitance, Abel and I embraced each other solidly, which was a rare show of affection, for me at least. Maybe in the moment, it was really the only sane thing to do.

"Brother Abel, how did you escape, what happened?" I eagerly enquired once we had disengaged ourselves.

"I was doing some late-night herb-gathering in the gardens, alone and humming to myself, when I heard the sounds of a terrible din coming from the castle. I thank the Gods that my eyes were spared the sight of what was happening, as the sounds were beyond anything I can describe. My gut instinct was to flee from those sounds, Marcus, not move towards them. I am not a warrior like you."

"I immediately started south in all haste, taking nothing with me but a basket of herbs. I am not as young and sprightly as I once was so had to slow my pace after a while and walk at a more manageable trot. I came upon this village early this morning, and whatever chaos had erupted at Carnagon was already at play when I arrived. I had little choice but to hide in a nearby copse of woods. I tried to block out the sounds, I know I should have helped, but…I am…"

I stepped forward and laid a hand on Brother Abel's broad shoulder as he allowed tears to overcome him. I offered the little consolation I could, "It's okay, Abel, I'm so glad you are still alive. Had you tried to save the villagers, I would be talking to your ghost right now. We will need you now more than ever."

Brother Abel controlled his weeping and looked at me with his reddened but earnest eyes. 'We, Marcus?'

"Yes, WE. There will be more survivors, I am sure. We will need to regroup and decide what to do next," I advised him, trying to offer my old friend the assurance and strength he so desperately needed.

Brother Abel nodded and even forced a smile. I smiled back and patted his arm before moving away to continue my check of the village. More bodies were strewn around the muddy streets, many bloodied and bearing gory-looking wounds. Some of the corpses were peppered with arrows, which the Utreshians had not considered to retrieve and take with them for reuse. This indicated to me that they were not wanting for supplies.

The worst corpse I came across was in a state of mutilation as the poor man's arm had been ripped off messily at the shoulder socket, as if with extreme animalistic strength. The man's rigid face was forever fixed in a hideous scream of death. A dark part of me imagined him screaming still from whatever afterlife awaits us, staggering around, armless and bloody, into nothingness. I squeezed my eyes and focused on the present. Morbid wondering would serve us little.

Brother Abel spent the next few hours going through the village alongside me, checking the various small gardens and allotments for anything we could eat, be it vegetable, fruit, grain, oat, leaf, plant or berry. We did come across a stable block, a sty and a barn, but any live animals had been stolen by the raiding party, or had wisely escaped to freedom. I found some minor comfort in knowing that at least the

Utreshian belly needed sustenance and had to be fed something. Any weakness would need to be exploited at that moment and there was no shame in it. The Utreshians had made it quite clear that there were no rules to this war and nothing was off the table. The manner of their attack went against any and all codes of valour known to Halians. I knew that we were dealing with beings little more than wild beasts when it came to morality and ethics, or lack thereof.

Brother Abel and I were sharing a loaf of bread with some cold meat and a bottle of half-drinkable wine when we spotted a small band of people moving towards the village. They were coming from the north, from the direction of Carnagon Castle. We had been silent for a while, each man in his own thoughts as they ate and drank, but we both stood as we registered this potential threat. From this distance, neither of our eyes could tell friend from foe, so we made the decision to conceal ourselves behind the cover of buildings until the newcomers came into proper view.

If it was foe, Abel and I agreed to head west to the thick cover of Lowgarth Forest, as travelling south or east presented flat, open land for miles in each direction where we would be totally exposed. Going back north would be like walking towards a chopping block or a hangman's noose, we both agreed.

As the walking party moved closer, I began to make out some features, one of which provided me with relief but the rest of which did not. The only relief was that the people were Halian folk, and I had no reason to see them as anything but kin. The closer they got, I realised that this was not some armed troop looking to restore order and offer stout resistance against the brutal invaders. These were outcasts and refugees like Abel and I. I could see that they were poorly clad, barely armed and carrying little on their backs. They kept their eyes to the ground and trudged forward with little sign of life, as if in keeping with the dead landscape around them.

As I saw the lead figure come more fully into view, my nightmare in the cell came back to me again. For the figure was that of Vincent Harbrandt, looking dishevelled and dirty, any nobility stripped from him. Brother Abel and I both moved forward into view, to offer a welcome to the new arrivals, if such a word can even be used. Vincent saw us but seemed to look straight through us with empty eyes, as if totally lost in a world of his own.

I stopped around 15 feet in front of the group, Brother Abel standing just off my right shoulder, hands clasped in front of his belly. Vincent had several retainers with him, looking little better than he did. I spotted that two of these retainers were transporting a simple stretcher with a figure lying still between them.

"Vincent, you're alive! How did you escape? Where's Elaine? I mean, where is Lady Harbrandt?" I enquired, more casually than I should have, but royal protocol be damned.

Vincent did not respond; he merely fixed me with a bleak stare as if something was broken beyond repair inside, before stepping to one side with his shoulders slumped. The retainers, two young guardsmen who had for whatever reason escaped the worst of the Utreshian onslaught, stepped forward a few paces to reveal their patient. At first, I saw a woman in a very poor state indeed. Her clothes were torn, hair tangled, face puffy and bloodied, breathing shallowly, sweating and ghostly pale, eyes closed against her hideous surroundings. I then noticed the dress she was wearing, and it was the same fine dress that had been gracing the noble form of Lady Harbrandt the fateful night before. The reality of it hit me like a hammer blow to the gut.

"Lady Harbrandt! Can you hear me?" I asked in a heightened and barely controlled voice.

It was then that Brother Abel stepped up and took temporary control of the situation. "Men, take Lady Harbrandt to that first home on the right with the plant pot by the front door, right now. I need to examine her."

The men seemed to wake up a little upon being addressed so directly and followed Brother Abel's directions towards the designated abode.

Whilst Brother Abel tended to Lady Harbrandt in the makeshift infirmary, I sat with Lord Harbrandt outside on a basic wooden bench. He had said few words since our reunion and preferred to sit with his hands clasped in his lap, pale-faced and staring at the ground with an air of resignation. He was clearly still in shock, but then started to gradually open up and unburden himself about the previous night's events. It was my turn to quieten and listen, although in truth I did not want to hear whatever he was going to say.

"It was whilst you were out of the room when this Lord Va'heash gave the order. I had noticed you having a word with one of your young trainees before making for the room's exit. I recall wondering where you were going, when there was a shift in the atmosphere, a tension that many of us could feel. I could see it in people's eyes and even…feel it in their very beings. The Utreshian retainers began slowly moving towards the guards, each picking a target, as if predetermined. The guards seemed none the wiser to their immediate pursuer, as they were probably watching the other retainers."

"Then it all happened so quickly and brutally; each retainer lunged at the guard with a short blade, which they must have concealed within their clothing. The retainers went straight for killing blows, plunging the blades deep into the guards' exposed necks, allowing horrific amounts of blood to pour freely across the floor."

At this point, Vincent paused, visibly shaken at having to relive this ghoulish ordeal and conjure up those images. I waited quietly for him to continue. After a few moments, he went on, "Most of the guards went to the ground without complaint and soon become still. The Utreshians were so fast and strong. A few of the tougher guards managed to evade the worst of the blows and instinctively fought back. One soldier, a tall trooper called Dalian, managed to break an Utreshian's teeth out with a solid punch, but other than a few other Halian retaliations, it was a one-sided battle. That huge giant, whatever the hell he is, knocked a soldier to the ground and stamped on his head which such force that…that the man's head exploded, like an egg being stomped on by an angry child. The innards of the man's head sprayed all over the clothes of nearby guests, but the beast itself seemed totally unfazed and just walked away, leaving monstrous bloody footprints over the boards. I'm sorry to be so graphic, Marcus, but you need to know who we're dealing with."

"Oh, I have a good idea about who we're dealing with. I was a guest of theirs in the dungeons and experienced their style of hospitality. Vincent, when I went back into the main hall once it had been taken over, Va'heash told me you and Lady Harbrandt had been taken away. He joked grimly about feeding you two to his hounds; at least I am glad you do not right now lie in the belly of whatever unthinkable four-legged creatures the Utreshians lead around on a leash. But…what happened though?" I enquired.

Vincent shakily resumed his story, and I feared that we were getting to the worst part. But I braced myself and listened.

"Elaine and I were grabbed roughly and marched out of the hall by a side entrance. A few of our braver nobles moved to our sides to try and defend us, and I will never forget those that did. Sadly, you can imagine what kind of chances they stood against the same brutish armed men who had just slaughtered armed castle guards with relative ease. I chose to remain quiet and not antagonise our captors unduly."

"But Elaine became spirited and began screaming to be unhanded. One of the Utreshians slapped her hard across the face, which silenced her demands. It also angered me enough to raise my voice in protest and warn the brute not to hit Lady Elaine, my sister and a leading Halian noble. This outburst of mine earned me a vicious strike to the stomach, one so hard that I felt like I folded in half. I could not move and felt as if I could not even breathe for several horrifying moments. I remember being carried up the stairs over an enormously broad shoulder, like a hunter carrying a dead fawn, before being dropped messily onto a carpeted floor."

"I became aware of a screaming female voice from the next room. Even in my state of pain and terror, I could recognise the desperate voice of my sister. She sounded like she was pleading, intermingled with bouts of barely controlled weeping. Events were clearly going against her, as her wailing only continued. It wasn't long before I heard the progress of several loud and heavy sets of feet going past my room and into hers. It was then that her screams stopped, as if whatever had appeared at the door had shocked her beyond any words."

"Then, I heard the heavy steps move further into the room, and Elaine's screaming picked up again. Only now…it was a different kind of screaming, one that I fear I will never be able to erase from my memory. A sound that no person should make. By now, I was banging on the wall in between us, yelling myself hoarse, telling Elaine that help was coming, although I knew it was a feeble lie. Marcus…I think they…they took turns with her."

Vincent screwed his eyes shut and tried to fight back tears. His face was a mask of pain and emotional agony. He shook his head before dropping it into his grimy hands.

"You don't need to go any further, Vincent. It's over now," I tried to console him. In all truth, nothing was over. The nightmare had hardly begun. However, that was not the truth Vincent needed to hear in that painful moment.

I did not tell him that Elaine would be okay. I had too much respect to lie to him like that. I had seen people in their dying state many times, and I knew when someone was soon to be moving to whatever lies beyond.

During this pause in our conversation, Brother Abel appeared at the door of the building, looking grim-faced and serious. We both looked at him from our shared bench, both wanting and not wanting to hear an update.

"Lord Harbrandt, please come in. Your sister would like a word with you."

Brother Abel and I waited quietly outside, with the other troops resting close by. We had all endured the roughest of nights and had earned an opportunity to gather ourselves. Brother Abel updated me on Lady Harbrandt's state whilst

Vincent shared some private moments with his beloved sister. These would sadly be the last moments they would ever share. Still, no man amongst us felt the need to state the inevitable.

"I have done all I can, Marcus, but her injury is too great for recovery to be possible. If I had treated her back in the infirmary with all my supplies and apparatus, it would have been a different story. I have tried to make her as comfortable as I can, given the circumstances," Brother Abel explained.

I started to speak, but refrained from passing comment before any words left my mouth. There was really nothing I could say.

We decided to bury Lady Harbrandt's body that afternoon, in that very village. The grave was dug under the shade of a large, sturdy oak tree, one that had not yet began to rot and wither as the smaller and newer trees had done. She had been wrapped in a fine linen rescued from one of the homes, only her pale face showing through the shroud, in a state of eternal sleep. We had no cleric with us, so no one could offer much of a final blessing. Brother Abel took it upon himself to conduct the short service. Vincent himself did not wish to make a comment at the time, a choice we respected and did not quarrel against.

Grief is an odd thing, and different people are affected in different ways. In later times, Vincent would reflect upon his sister's life, but it was not that day. As the seven of us stood around that grave listening to Brother Abel's consoling words, I felt that an invisible bond had been established between us. We seven were somehow going to be the first of the next step. There was Brother Abel and myself, Vincent, and the four guards who had accompanied Vincent; their first names were Gustav, Peter, Saul and Mordak. Whatever was going to happen next, it was starting right then.

I knew that we could not loiter at that village of Otter's Wall for too long. The jaws of the Utreshian forces had already passed us and we assumed that they would continue to head south. I did not know how well the Utreshian invaders knew the land of Halia, but their familiarity with it would be growing by the hour as more scouting and foraging parties spread out and took stock of the place. We had to compact the useful equipment we had found during our search of Otter's Wall, arm ourselves with the best weapons available, and make a move south.

Even with seven men, five of them trained fighters, we were still no match for anything more than a few Utreshian stragglers. Even a small unit would make easy work of us. We were lightly armoured and the only weapons we had found were primitive farm tools in varying states of ill repair. The residents of Otter's Wall had not been wealthy people and therefore owned little of value.

For our move south, we all knew that we would have to choose our route carefully. Walking out in the open during daylight, or what passed for daylight under the murky sky, would be unwise. We did not know what eyes were watching us. After some discussion in the tavern, which we had commandeered as our makeshift headquarters, we decided that the best option was to travel on the outskirts of Lowgarth Forest, just inside the cover of trees. We dared not travel inside the forest proper as ghoulish tales of the forest's dwellers had reached our ears during tales around the campfire, or in the favoured alehouse just outside the castle walls.

Hardened travellers who had trod the span of Halia told haunting tales of giant wolves and bears in the forest, thick furred beasts with evil eyes and rows of flesh-tearing teeth. It was rumoured that the largest bear of the forest could not even be killed by sword, spear or arrow, and had lived deep within the forest for over 500 years. A beast so fearsome that men could be rendered deaf just being in earshot of its roar, and so savage that it could enclose 4 grown men within its vast drooling jaws. I say 'it' as none were able to say whether the beast was male or female.

Our band of seven was about to set off in a south-west direction at dusk, baggage packed and distributed as evenly and fairly as we could, when we were alerted to a new arrival. Gustav, who had been working sentry duty whilst the rest of us finalised the packing, yelled to us from just outside the tavern entrance, "Lone person approaching, looks like a young lad. I think I recognise the kid actually."

I paused my activities vto respond to Gustav's warning and see who was approaching. I picked up the sickle I had selected as my new weapon of choice, before leaving the tavern. If the worst came to the worst, I would not die empty handed! I spotted the figure almost immediately and felt my heart lift as I recognised the face of young Simon Fester.

I found myself running forward to greet Simon, and for the second time that day, I embraced one of my comrades. We held the embrace for a moment, and then held Simon's shoulders and looked into his face. I did not know whether to laugh or cry, so ended up doing a little of both at the same time.

"Simon, what happened? Those bastards told me you were dead, that they'd hung you in the courtyard!"

Simon shook his head and grinned, before responding, "As you can see, I'm quite well, Captain. We need to leave now though, there is a 30-strong squad of those big bastards coming this way, not two miles away."

Within minutes, our new and strengthened band of eight fellows was moving out towards the dark realm of Lowgarth. We had thought to fire the village before fleeing, to deny the Utreshians any further resources or any place to recuperate, but decided against it due to time constraints. I walked alongside Simon, listening keenly to his recount of last night's hectic events.

"I managed to escape down that tunnel you showed me and get out of the castle through that small door. I got chased for a bit outside the walls, but I knew where I was going and those Utreshian fucks didn't! Took a while but I managed to lose them. When that curtain dropped down, my first thought was to cut through and help you, but you did give me an order to run, Captain."

"I did, Simon, and I'm glad you did run. It wasn't cowardice, you know that, don't you?"

"Yeah, I know. I felt cowardly at first, but had I stayed, they may well have just slaughtered me for fun. I'm guessing they kept you alive for possible information, Captain? They had no reason to spare me, in that sense," Simon responded.

"That's about the long and the short of it, Simon," I confirmed.

We both walked in silence for a fair while. Each man was likely lost in his own thoughts about the path ahead. I believe we all felt fear as the darkness and foreboding of the forest loomed up to meet us, as if to swallow us. I would doubt the sanity of any man who was not fearful. Our period in Otter's

Wall had allowed the men some rest, so now our plan was to walk throughout the night, pausing now and again to catch our breath and rest our legs. We would sleep during the day, as to venture out during these hours seemed nothing but folly.

As we finally entered the outskirts of the ancient forest, it was like entering another realm, a dark and mysterious one which could provide endless terrors the deeper you travelled. Gustav remarked to us that he had spotted a tall man-like being climbing the trees with ease, and even standing still on the tree trunk, as if defying gravity, before disappearing. Peter told us that he had seen several sets of glowing eyes watching our progress from the deep foliage.

I told them to stay alert and focus on the path ahead, for if we were attacked, we would defend ourselves as best we could. I myself took care not to look too deep into that darkness, or I would also see something, whether it was there or not. I would not invite my eyes and fear to play tricks on me. I needed to stay in control.

Our path lit by several small torches, we walked just within the forest boundary for around 10 miles that first long night, stopping only a few times. At each stop, we shared a little food and the small amount of drinkable water salvaged from the wrecked homes of Otter's Wall. We spoke little, not only for reasons of remaining undetected to possible nearby Utreshian ears, but also because none of us felt like talking.

At daybreak, when the sky turned from a roiling grey-brown to the usual sickly yellow, we decided to make camp and get what sleep we could. We were all downbeat, fatigued and afraid to some measure; however, Peter was especially anxious, and my attempts to calm him were proving unsuccessful. I put Peter somewhere in his mid-twenties and did not need a mystic to tell me that Peter was not experienced in any real manner of battle. He came across as a man, a boy rather, who had been pampered growing up.

"I can't stay in this fucking forest a moment longer, Marcus. I can hear voices calling in my head. This place is bloody evil. I'm gonna go crazy if we stay here much longer," Peter protested, his voice quavering and eyes wide with fright.

"We're all afraid, Peter, nothing wrong with that. But we can't just go walking across the open land just yet. We're sitting ducks out there and you know it. Look, let's bed down now and by tomorrow we should be able to turn into Valmere Valley until—"

My explanation was broken by Peter's shrill outburst, "TOMORROW, FUCKING TOMORROW? I can't stay another minute in this place. I'm going to take my chances out there. You folks do what you want!"

With that final line, Peter turned and hurriedly dashed out of the forest, carrying nothing. We watched in dismay as he fled out into the scrubland that had until fairly recently been tended fields. He did not slow down or look back once.

There was an uncomfortable silence, which was broken somewhat jovially by Gustav, "Oh well, that's one less mouth to feed. He wasn't much of a soldier anyway."

Gustav's remark was likely meant as something of jest, but no one broke a smile. It was then that Brother Abel spoke up, "Poor Peter, he ran off without food, water or even a weapon. He won't last long. What if he is caught and questioned and gives away our location? Shouldn't we go after him?"

I turned to Brother Abel and answered him, more sternly than I should have, but I could not let the party come apart now. "No, we will do no such thing. Simon made a choice to flee the relative safety of the party. He is on his own now. We will take turns to watch out for possible intruders, whether from within or outside of the forest. If any danger encroaches then we will be sure to up and move, and fight if need be. I have no intention of those Utreshian dogs taking me alive again."

The rest of the men were quietly watching the heated exchange between Abel and I and no one had anything to add. Abel himself nodded grimly and turned his eyes to the ground, not willing to argue his point any further.

"Mordak, could you take the first watch shift, please? After 2 hours, wake me up and I will take the next watch," I requested rather than ordered. I was not officially in charge of these men out here and did not want to overstep my mark or be seen talking down to men who were currently very important to me. Lord Vincent Harbrandt was the highest-ranking member of the party by far, in terms of nobility and status at least. However, he had been silent and walking head down for almost the entire journey since leaving Otter's Wall. He was in no state to command and keep together a band of fighting men under such strained circumstances.

As Mordak prepared himself for his watch, which included stretching his broad, muscular limbs and slapping his face to wake himself up, the rest of us prepared our bedding and tried to get comfortable in the undergrowth of the forest floor.

I slept fitfully that day, despite being so tired. Once again, my mind wandered in bleak nightmares of a ravaged and plague-ridden land of despair. I saw fellow Halians fettered in chains and being force-marched down a road, spurred on by the brutal whips and sticks of large Utreshian brutes. In my nightmares, the Utreshians were terrifying giants, who looked down upon their chattel with glowing red eyes. I saw bodies impaled messily on spikes, in various states of mutilation. I felt true despair as those nightmares ravaged my sleep and denied me any real rest. It was almost a relief when Mordak poked me awake after his 2-hour stint. It was from one nightmare into another really, but at least in the nightmare of reality, I felt slightly more in control.

Finally, the day was over, the dark was descending, and it was time to regain our feet and carry on progressing south. My plan was to continue until we reached the relative cover of Valmere Valley, whereby we could turn east and cut across the land using the cover of natural geographic features. I knew there to be various caverns dotted around the rocky parts of that valley which we could use for some much-needed shelter. This was the plan I had tried to communicate to Peter, just before he fled. I had shared this plan with the rest of the group, who had raised no objection, primarily as no one could devise any wiser plan under the circumstances.

That second night of walking was very similar to the first, only we were one fewer. This did, as Gustav had mentioned, mean that food went that bit further; however, we were one fighting man fewer and each lookout would have to stay alert that bit longer. The mood was still downbeat and the men quiet and lost in their own thoughts. Vincent still spoke little, despite Brother Abel's several attempts to get him to open up. His state of being was very understandable, given that not only was he stripped of his former nobility and wandering through dark woods at night like some vagabond, but he had the added trauma of hearing his sister being brutalised and witnessing her untimely and unjust death. At least he had taken some food and drink and was still on his feet. I wanted to tell him to keep faith, to stay strong so that he could avenge his sister's death, but I never found the right words or moment to convey what sounded to me at least like sage advice.

After what felt to be an age of endless walking, we came in sight of the top of the hill which sloped down into Valmere Valley, which would be the next stint of our route south. My plan deep in my mind was to reach the solid outpost of Mirgot's Pass, which acted as a final barrier before a traveller, friend, foe or invader entered the Golden City of Farchester. Once past Mirgot's Pass, an invading army were almost home free, as the city itself was not as well-defended as in previous years. Many of the fighting men were campaigning in foreign lands, which weakened the fighting strength of the city at home.

This alone may not have been a huge issue; however, it was complemented by the fact that due to poor craftsmanship and cost-cutting, a large portion of the castle wall had tumbled down not four days prior to the sacking of Carnagon Castle. It was clear that Va'heash had an inside informer, but at that time, we had no inkling of who the perpetrator was. There had also been an outbreak of 'Devil's Curse', a virulent disease which spread easily amongst the common areas of the city, due to the closely packed houses and poorer sanitation. Whether this disease was just circumstance or engineered by one of Va'heash's lackeys, we were unsure of at the time.

This was information that I had overheard from a Farchester contact of mine only the night before, whilst drinking a few ales at the 'Lannister's Lion' just outside

Carnagon. It was only that night, when the castle was attacked, that I started to fit the pieces together.

I had been careful about how much of this information I shared with the soldiers, as I did not want to alarm them or break their spirits even further by telling them what a sorry state Farchester was in. I did not even know how we would reach Mirgot's Pass, as it still lay many miles to the south, through desolate wasteland and—I had every reason to assume—a strong Utreshian presence. I was directing the group one step at a time.

I was in the lead, with Brother Abel walking in tandem with Vincent Harbrandt, once again trying to encourage some gentle conversation. Next came Gustav, walking with his rusty and chipped sword firmly in his right hand, almost as if anticipating what was about to occur. Next came Saul, who had chosen to adopt a pair of short-handled wood-axes as fighting weapons.

Mordak, the tallest and strongest of out small party, walked behind Saul, a large blacksmith's hammer resting against his broad back, but ready to be taken in his large hands whenever necessary. Young Simon brought up the rear and was carrying the same castle-forged longsword he had managed to escape Carnagon Castle with. I, of course, still carried my sickle, although had no idea how it would handle against flesh, or armour. Chopping through soft wheat was hardly like chopping through steel.

I quietly gave the order that we were to leave the cover of the forest and proceed smartly downhill into the valley. I could see the relief on the men's faces, without exception. Not one of them wanted to remain in the forest any longer than necessary. I led our party of seven out of the cover of

Lowgarth Forest just as the day was breaking and more of the desolate landscape was revealed by what little sunlight could penetrate the sickly fog high above us.

The start of the valley was only half a mile in an easterly direction, and I wanted the group to move quickly into its relative cover. We were making the distance in goodish time, not as smartly as I hoped for, but I could not exactly beat the men into moving faster. We were all tired, and Brother Abel was not as sprightly as he once was. However, we were leaving no one behind; I would not abandon Brother Abel any more than I would abandon my own mother or father.

We were almost within throwing distance of the start of the valley when I could tell that trouble was afoot and our makeshift weapons were about to be tested. A number of figures had crested a hill not 300 metres away. From this distance, our eyes could not really tell friend from foe. I believe that we all saw these figures appear at roughly the same time; Gustav called out, "Who are those figures up there? There's about ten of 'em."

"If they are the enemy, we cannot afford an open battle. Double time down into the valley. If they are friends, then…"

My instructions were promptly halted as the bone-chilling sound of a huge roar reached our ears from across that 300-metre span. A deep, ferocious sound that no man could make. If this was not indication enough that the newcomers were indeed foes, this fact was reinforced when the ten or so men began to angrily charge down the slope towards our small, exposed party. The men moved faster than any of us would have liked. They were likely fresh, and I could see that they possessed serious armour and weaponry as they began to close the gap. I gave the only order I could, "RUN! Run for the valley!"

We all picked up the pace as best we could; however, despite literally running for his life, poor Brother Abel could not bring his body to move as fast as the rest of us, who were younger and in better physical shape. Abel pleaded with the rest of us to leave him and save ourselves, such was his selfless character, but I was damned if I would take his advice.

I knew that we would not make it to any kind of shelter before the Utreshian war party was upon us. We would have to fight—win, lose or die. I would not get cut down like a scared rabbit running for its life; if death was certain then I would rather meet it fighting. I quickly gave a new order, "Stop, form a line, me in the centre and three to either side. Defensive stance and strike only if attacked."

Amazingly, no one continued fleeing in desperation as I feared they would. I felt some small pride that the sound of my voice could inspire men to stand against certain death! I took the centre as agreed, with Abel directly to my right, then young Simon, then Gustav on the right flank. Saul stood firmly to my left, both axes ready for blood if it came to it. Vincent stood to Saul's left, now brandishing a two-pronged hay fork in his shaking hands. Vincent was no warrior and had only held a sword in practice and games; however, if he could somehow turn his rage into anger, then he stood a chance. That fork could drop even a big Utreshian if even one of the wicked prongs found his exposed eyes. I knew that they could be killed as Simon and I had committed that feat in tandem. Mordak took the left flank, his large hammer held out diagonally across his chest, to protect against attack rather than deal it out.

We planted our feet and stood as the Utreshians rushed towards us. There was no best way to intercept an attack where we were outnumbered by superior warriors, at least in terms of equipment and brute strength. The Utreshians did not simply barrel into us like angry bulls, as I was preparing for, but instead drew up around 10 feet away. It was clear that they were not mindless barbarians despite their savage capabilities.

A leading warrior stepped forward from the Utreshian pack. He was tall and powerfully built with what I classed as medium-strength armour. This was likely a fast-moving scouting party, so unencumbered with the heavier protection that many of his comrades would be garbed in. The armour, which looked like some unknown dark metal fashioned into chain-links worn over tough animal-hide clothing, would be enough to protect him from the worst of any damage inflicted by tools designed for farming or smithing. The leader's face was scarred, grim-looking and serious. I could tell from the outset that this was a warrior who had experienced many battles and could carve up living flesh like most of us carve up a juicy steak.

It seemed that these Utreshians wanted to talk first, and I sensed some ultimatum incoming. Our group still braced their weapons readily, I had given no order for them to be lowered.

"You do not need to die, although I have no qualms about killing you. Drop your weapons and you will be taken hostage," the leader commanded in a guttural and unpleasant-sounding voice, although I could not fault his pronunciation of our Halian language.

"Taken hostage to where, to whom?" I retorted, pushing my luck, but I would not submit to this foreign invader so meekly.

"Drop…your…weapons…now," enforced the Utreshian leader, as if speaking to an imbecile. It was clear that his bloodlust would not be kept in check much longer. His eyes were already betraying the beast that was preparing to pounce. He was done with this conversation, if it could even be classed as that. The Utreshian scout leader was merely issuing an instruction—take it or leave it.

I do not know how much longer I would have stood there, not wanting to submit but hesitant to get everyone slaughtered, had we not experienced the greatest gift of luck ever experienced. We heard a glorious chorus of bold battle cries coming from the east, from the valley. We all turned, Halian and Utreshian alike, to see the inspiring sight of a party of Halian troops coming to our aid. I immediately spotted at least three mounted troops and maybe five foot soldiers charging across the land with weapons raised. I took immediate advantage of this moment and opened our attack with a vicious swipe at the unprotected neck of the Utreshian leader.

The Utreshian leader had fast reflexes, but not quite fast enough. As he drew his head back instinctively, the long reach of my sickle bit deep enough into his flesh for blood to flow out. First blood had been drawn and battle had commenced. The rest of the Utreshians surged forward, growling and ready for some slaughter. I slashed once again at the leader's eyes as his hands instinctively clutched his throat to stem the blood. My strike struck true, as the leader staggered back, now blinded as well as choking. At least that was the leader wounded, but not yet down.

I jerked my head to my right to witness Gustav parry an Utreshian sword blow before following up with a vicious downward strike at the enemy's lightly protected head. Gustav's sword may not have been in the best shape, but it seemed that the strike was enough to stun his enemy and drop him to his knees. Simon, who was the best armed of all of us, was displaying impressive martial prowess as he went toe-to-toe with a larger Utreshian, armed with the usual ugly-looking blades that Utreshians seemed to favour. Simon lacked strength, but his agility and speed was besting that of the Utreshian. After several exchanged blows, Simon managed to sever the Utreshian at the thick wrist of his right hand, disabling the enemy enough for Simon to finish the job with a direct sword thrust though the armpit and into where he hoped the Utreshian's heart lay. Simon dragged his gore-slicked sword out of the brute's body, panting with excursion and adrenaline.

"Well done, lad!" I roared out to Simon, who nodded back at me, eyes alight and grinning.

I turned my head left to check on the progress of that flank, and immediately noticed several bloodied bodies lying still on the dirt, both Halian and Utreshian. I did not have time to work out who it was, for I spotted a wicked-looking cleaver come flying towards my head. I managed to raise my arms and bring the sickle into a defensive position, which caught the worst of the blow, but dropped me to my knees and caused my arms to scream in pain. Without any real thought, I unlocked the blade and quickly slashed at the Utreshian's exposed ankles, causing the enemy to yell and join me on his knees. I was about to finish the job with another neck strike, but the kneeling Utreshian was knocked flat violently as a hefty Halian stallion crashed into him. I was pretty sure I heard his neck break under the impact.

The timely arrival of the Halian horsemen ended any chance the Utreshians had, as the riders moved around the melee at speed, striking down relentlessly at the heads, shoulders and necks of the Utreshians. The whole ordeal must have only lasted a few minutes; however, in the thick of it, it had felt to me like much longer. With all the Utreshians now dead or dying, it was time to take stock of the losses and regain some order.

My first instinct was to see who we had lost, who those Halian bodies lying on the ground were. We had sadly lost Saul, who lay face-up, staring blankly into the heavens. He had taken a blade deep in his chest, causing a messy wound. However, it was some comfort that he had marked his enemy before going down, as both of his wood-axes were lathered with enemy blood, which I then noticed was actually a toxic-looking green and not the crimson red of Halian folk. Mordak was wounded and lay prone, but was still in the land of the living, although semi-conscious with the extent of the injury. His left leg had been gashed open by an enemy blade, but had missed any major artery.

"He will live if we can get him medical treatment soon."

I craned my head upwards to see the red face of brother Abel staring down at me intently. I agreed with this diagnosis, although at that moment I had little idea as to where said medical treatment would be procured from. We were still in the middle of nowhere.

"Is that you, Marcus Kane?"

I stood up to address the speaker, who was still mounted, and recognised my old comrade and battle brother, Kurt Winters. Kurt and I had served together in several campaigns, side by side, and had saved each other's lives more than once. It was truly a joy to see him again, despite the circumstances.

Kurt dismounted his horse and approached me, smiling broadly through his blood-splattered but unharmed face. We did not embrace in front of all the men, but clasped hands firmly, something of a formal battleground greeting we had established.

"Kurt, I am at a loss for words. Once again, I owe you my life, OUR lives." I extended my arm to introduce our small fellowship, who all looked at Kurt and nodded in appreciation and greeting.

"But where did you come from, Kurt? Why were you out here in Valmere Valley with such a small group of soldiers?" I enquired of Kurt.

"Your friend managed to find us and told us your story so far. We travelled the valley towards Lowgarth Forest, hoping that we'd come across your little band. We were just coming uphill when we heard that monstrous Utreshian roar and figured that it was most likely you they were roaring at," Kurt explained.

It was then that Peter came into view, the same Peter who had fled from Lowgarth Forest in fear. I honestly did not know whether to strike him or bow down and thank him for saving us from a terrible fate. Simon himself looked slightly uncertain, as if he read my conflicting emotions. I actually made neither of those gestures, but simply thanked Simon for his aid.

"That's okay, Captain. Sorry for running off like that, but my panic got the better of me. I was wrong to flee," came Simon's genuine-sounding apology.

I accepted his apology before turning back to Kurt, who spoke first, "Marcus, gather your men and follow me down into the valley. We have established a small but concealed base which I pray is safe from Utreshian eyes. There is more of us than what you see here."

So it seemed that we were a small group no longer. I felt in that moment that we had entered the next stage of our retaliation, our resistance.

Kurt led our band downhill into the valley. Two of the fresher Halian troops from Kurt's band kindly agreed to carry the injured Mordak between them on a makeshift stretcher, whilst the body of poor Saul, who had died valiantly, was wrapped in a cloth and laid over the broad back of one of the strong horses. Luckily, there were no other serious injuries suffered amongst the group, only cuts, bruises and sprains that would heal in time.

Kurt stopped by what appeared to be a random patch of vegetation, before uttering in a low voice the phrase 'the salmon swim upriver in summer'. At first, I wondered what Kurt was playing at and thought that this was a strange time to be jesting. However, after only a momentary pause, the vegetation parted, revealing a narrow entrance to a dark passage. Two alert sentries stood either side of the passage, eyes keen and spears held to attention. Kurt led us into the passage quietly and we progressed two abreast into the gloomy tunnel. Just before going in, I turned my head to scour briefly for any unwelcome eyes which may be observing us, but could not immediately see anything unusual.

Once inside the main cavern of what appeared to be a network of smaller caves and tunnels, I looked around at the assembled residents. The light was produced by several lit torches blazing against the solid rock walls, which cast shadows across the area. Several trestle tables had been set up in the main space, upon which people now sat, doing different activities, from drinking ale, to writing on parchment by candlelight, to playing games on a wooden board.

The cavern ceiling ended some six feet above my head, so at least there was some feeling of space. The residents seemed to be a mix of all folk—soldiers, washerwomen, younger children, farmers, feeble old folk who lay huddled in furs, clerics, and various types of healers. I noticed that Brother Abel greeted another stout-looking fellow clad in robes similar to Abel himself. The two shared a quiet but animated conversation at one of the tables.

I also spotted a familiar face amongst the crowd, that of Robert Howlett, a farmer by trade, but also something of an unofficial leader amongst the common folk. Robert's was a voice that carried weight. I was about to go and greet Robert when I heard Kurt's voice behind me, "Marcus, follow me. We have a lot to discuss."

Kurt led me down a tunnel off from the main cavern, into a smallish area which had clearly been shaped painstakingly with tools into something like an office. There was even a rug gracing the cold stone floor and small tapestries adorning the walls. A rectangular table stood in the centre of the room. Several men stood up as Kurt and I entered; I recognised none of them.

"Gentlemen, may I introduce Captain Marcus Kane? Marcus ran the castle guard at Carnagon, up until recently at least," Kurt explained to the standing members of this special meeting, before continuing: "Marcus, may I introduce Lord Hartwright of Galverly Green? Bishop Edgeforth, head of the

Apollatian church, and lastly, my second-in-command, David Stire."

Each of the three men bowed their heads as they were introduced and maintained eye contact with me. I knew nothing of these men and only had Kurt's judgement to rely on that they could be trusted with what would be very sensitive conversation. In my personal view, the title of 'Lord' no longer automatically inspired respect after Va'heash had played his wicked hand. The church and the Gods they worshipped clearly didn't help much and seemed content to sit and watch from on high.

However, I could tell that David was a fighting brother and must have proven himself to reach the level of Kurt's right-hand man. I knew that Kurt demanded high standards and was a good judge of character, or at least I still hoped that he was, standing there looking at three strangers.

"Marcus, please join us at the table," Kurt offered, indicating a basic wooden chair at one end of the table. Kurt looked around the room, as if reading my mind, before explaining something about where we were, "We have been utilising this cavern system for many years now, Marcus. We have extended it, tooled it and shaped it into something of both a second home and a military outpost. Whilst Halia has never experienced an invasion of this kind, we always knew that someday it would happen, and did not want to be helpless when it did. I don't know how much you know about Halia's underground tunnel system," Kurt explained.

"I know of its existence, but don't know any real specifics or anything. I have never seen any maps or prints of it," I responded, quite truthfully.

"I'm not sure if anyone knows of its full extent, in terms of just how many miles of tunnels there are, how deep they go, where they start and stop, whether they are safe, whether what is there is flooded, whether there is any access to clean water or safety down there, or even what lifeforms lurk down there. The first tunnels were rumoured to have been carved by ancient Halians some 700 years ago, roughly 200 feet below surface level, but of course, tunnels can be deeper or shallower than that," Kurt continued.

I nodded, trying to take in all of this information, before Lord Hartwright leaned forward slightly, his green eyes inquisitive, and addressed me: "Captain Kane, sorry to interrupt these proceedings, but I am very keen to know what happened at Carnagon Castle. Could you brief us now, if it's not too much trouble?"

I looked at Kurt, who nodded his approval, before I turned back to Lord Hartwright and started recounting the harrowing events of the last few days. I began with the feast, mentioning how I had been kept in the dark about the guests and exactly why they were visiting the castle. I moved on to the intrusion though the cellar trapdoor and the violent massacre in the main hall. I then detailed my confinement in the castle cells and unpleasant escape through the sewer system. I took the listeners through my journey to Otter's Wall, how I had met up with Brother Abel and then intercepted Lord Harbrandt and his small group.

I informed the group about the tragic death of Lady Harbrandt, but did not go into any detail about what she had suffered beforehand. I finished with the oppressive and bleak trek through Lowgarth Forest before leaving for the relative safety of Valmere Valley, which was where Kurt picked up the story.

There was a silence in the room as the men digested my tale, before Bishop Edgeforth tentatively posed a sensitive question, his lined face a mask of concern, "You mentioned the deeply saddening death of our beloved Lady Harbrandt; how is Lord Vincent taking the loss, may I ask?"

"He was in a state of shock for some while, Bishop Edgeforth. He said little and ate little. However, I believe that he is very slowly regaining something of his former self. I regret to tell you that Vincent is forever changed though; I saw it in his eyes."

"I think we will ALL be changed by this in some way, Captain Kane," Lord Hartwright opined.

I was curious about how Kurt and his group had come to be in this place, especially with several horses and properly equipped troops. It was now time for me to hear his recounting. Kurt freely told me his tale.

"The Utreshians did not bother with the 'Trojan Horse' business at Barford Castle. The place is nowhere near as strong or significant as Carnagon. No, they just attacked at night with a huge force and tried to overwhelm us with poor steel and savagery. They managed to take the ramparts with long ladders and plenty of fearlessness, despite the pounding that my men gave them. Before long, my men were nigh wiped out and I gave the order to retreat with as much order as possible, which was not much given the life or death situation we were in."

"I know not about the Utreshians you faced, but the beasts that attacked us bared fangs, like a wild dog, and their eyes glowed red in the darkness. They are not men like us, Marcus.

We cannot fight them their way, they will keep beating us back. Anyway, I led around 20 men to this hidden outpost, although now slightly less hidden."

So, Kurt had at least faced the foe in real battle prior to the minor scuffle earlier in the day. There was one question I had to ask Kurt though, regarding a phrase he had uttered during his explanation.

"Kurt, you mentioned a 'Trojan Horse', what does that mean?" I enquired.

"Oh, it's something from an old story about ancient Gre…Never mind. It's not important. It's just a saying for when intruders enter their enemy's region disguised as something harmless, or even friendly," Kurt explained helpfully.

"Well, one thing is for certain; we are going to have to enter this tunnel system one way or another. Moving south during the day or even the night across open land is madness. We cannot even travel through Lowgarth Forest any longer, even if we wanted to, as it turns towards the mountains and we do not have the means to traverse those," I ventured.

There was a pause as each man seemed to contemplate the next step in his own mind, rather than speak too quickly and risk uttering something foolish. Kurt then stood up and brought the meeting to a close: "Well, at least this discussion has been helpful in summarising how we got here and possible plans going forward. I will be holding separate meetings over the next few days to finalise a plan of action. I will call for you gentlemen in good time if you are required. In the meantime, get some proper rest, Marcus, and regain your strength. There is plenty of good food here and beds for you and your men. It is so good to see you, my old friend." Kurt explained, finishing with one of his trademark semi-smiles.

I stood up and bowed to the party, before taking my leave.

I took Kurt's advice and spent some time recuperating and replenishing my body with clean water tapped from an underground brook, and wholesome food from the larder. I joined Brother Abel, Simon and Vincent as we sat together at one of the spare benches and filled our bellies with beef, bread and a hearty soup. During this time, I spoke with my immediate group of men to see how they were faring. Just because we had become part of a larger group and were no longer taking turns to guard each other's lives in the dark woods, it did not mean that I didn't care about them or value their kinship. I knew that there were struggles up ahead and we would need to be close again. Standing shoulder to shoulder against a battle that would be happening in some form, at some stage, whether we liked it or not.

I was encouraged to see that my old friend Vincent was talking more, eating, resting and even breaking the odd smile. I was encouraged to see that some fire and life was coming back into him. I knew that I would need to put him through some basic weapons training, although I could not find the right moment to pose the question. Vincent Harbrandt was still a lord of Halia, and the residents of the outpost felt hesitant about issuing orders to a man who had always been the one to do the ordering. I knew Vincent better, so did not have quite the same hang-ups about speaking more directly to senior nobility.

It was two days after my meeting with Kurt, Lord Hartwright and Bishop Edgeforth, when I was once again summoned to that same furnished chamber. It was harder to keep time when almost constantly underground; however, I know that it was roughly midday when I sat down in that same worn chair. This time however, I was in the company of Kurt and one other person, the farmer and unofficial leader of the common people, Robert Howlett. I had not seen Robert since that first day in the main cavern.

"Marcus, you already know Robert Howlett, so I can skip the business of introductions," Kurt spoke.

"No, Robert and I are well met. It's good to see you alive and reasonably well, Robert," came my amiable greeting.

"Likewise, Marcus. I knew those Utreshian dogs could not kill a true Halian like yourself quite so easily," Robert said with a chuckle.

"They failed to kill me. Sadly, a lot of other 'true Halians' lie dead, their bodies dumped into a ditch like they were garbage," I retorted, not aware of how terse it sounded. The horrific vision of the filth-covered corpses in the ditch came back to me with a vengeance. I could almost smell that horrid odour again, even though Carnagon was by now some 40 miles north.

"I'm sorry, Marcus. I don't mean to speak light of their deaths. Many good people have already been slain as part of this invasion. They will always be remembered," Robert consoled gently, not meeting my eyes.

Kurt waited for the uncomfortable moment to pass before continuing with the purpose of this small meeting: "I invited you both here as Robert has managed to attain what we believe to be the most up-to-date maps of the tunnel system which runs under Halia. Note that 'up-to-date' does not necessarily mean 'accurate'. No one knows of any accurate maps of the tunnels, or what such maps would even look like were they found. I'm afraid that even with the maps, there will be some rerouting and playing by the ear.

"There will no doubt be cave-ins, blockages, floods and other such obstructions which are not present on the map. That cannot be helped, I'm afraid. We will have to make do with the resources available to us," Kurt directed, before addressing Robert, "Robert, could you please direct Marcus and I to the nearest entrance to the tunnel system, and also I wonder if you have managed to carve out a possible route to Mirgot's Pass?" Kurt enquired.

Robert spread the map open on the meeting table, peering at it intently with his deep-set brown eyes. The map looked to be slightly dog-eared around the edges and faded. I did not even want to ask how old it was. It was an irrelevant question and honestly, it was another thing that I felt better not knowing.

"The nearest entrance is right here, 3 miles away as the crow flies. I have eyes on the ground which confirm that the entrance, which is simply and unimaginatively titled 'Door 22', is still there and affords access to the tunnels," Robert detailed, indicating with a thick truncheon-like finger where Door 22 was on the map.

Robert then proceeded to take Kurt and I through a possible route he had already traced out. The total distance of what then became known officially as 'Robert's route' was somewhere between 15 and 16 miles. Upon hearing that number, I felt myself losing courage right there in that chamber. 15 miles across open ground was nothing to a healthy and mobile solider, even carrying fighting and field equipment. However, that same distance in dark tunnels, where any number of difficulties could arise, was an entirely different challenge. It was one that we had to face though, there was little alternative. We could not hide underground like mice whilst the invading murderers ravaged the lands and broke down the doors to beautiful Farchester.

"Thank you for this information, Robert. This right now is invaluable. I have a further question though; one you may not be able to answer. Are we likely to find any resistance down there? I mean, do you know what may be…living…down there?" I enquired of Robert.

"Oh, well. The only information I can tell you, Marcus, is mainly just tales I've heard over the years. One old man, now long dead, told me over a pint of ale that he had travelled the roads from Door 24 to Door 27 during his youth, which is near to the route we plan to take. The old fellow spoke of meeting, and having to overcome, a large wolf-like creature. Apparently, ten men engaged with this creature, and only the storyteller and two other soldiers were left breathing once the creature lay dead on the cold stone ground, its body covered in sword stabs and cuts. Bear in mind that this old fellow was recounting a tale from long before. The details may have become fuzzy, plus the old fellow may have been a little creative with the story, as if to entertain more than inform.

"Other than that, I have heard the usual gossip about enormous rats the size of cats who could chew through human bones like it was nothing. Huge dog-sized spiders who would crawl out of the dark before plunging toxic fangs into a poor man's flesh. Oddly enough, no one has ever managed to retrieve the body of such a being. I feel more likely that they are myths, which sound good around a campfire after a few ales."

Robert paused, before his face took on a more serious note. He continued, "There is however a more recent and better-documented story, one that has more grounding than a large wolfman killing seven armed soldiers. This story concerns the apparent fate of a real Halian soldier, a man from Farchester named Teryn Mooden. According to the clerk's records which are, or I hope still are, housed securely at the Bathington Library, Mooden was amongst a team of ten soldiers sent to clear and secure a route between Doors 5 and 8 of the tunnels. The record states that this effort was in preparation for a shipment of minerals, too unwieldy and cumbersome to transport at surface level. Once the tunnels were cleared, the minerals were transported safely to Door 8, where they were lifted to the surface by a pulley system, which may or may not still be functioning. This record dates back only 8 years 4 months. This information can be verified."

"However, what is a matter of debate is precisely what happened *after* the task was completed. For when both minerals and soldiers had been safely transported back to the surface, it was noted that Mooden, who had been bringing up the rear of the party down in the tunnels, was strangely absent. Realising Mooden's absence, the group leader ordered two of the soldiers to go straight back to Door 8 and see if they could locate Mooden."

"Both soldiers went back and re-entered Door 8, before proceeding to the top of the elevator shaft and shouting Mooden's name down into the inky darkness. But what came next is where the later statements of the soldiers differ, as 'soldier one', forgive me but no name is listed in the statement sheet, stated that he heard no response at all, just an eerie silence. However, the man known only as 'soldier two' stated something very different. He told the investigating officer that he heard an inhuman scream echoing and bouncing up the elevator shaft from the blackness. A scream that he could not believe came from a human throat, no matter how scared the issuer of the scream was. He also stated that he looked down into the darkness and spotted two large red lights, which he could not explain, as they did not leave any torches lit down there. When asked by the officer if the red lights could have been eyes, soldier two just shook his head and screwed his eyes shut, as if he did not want to speculate on such a reality."

"So, already there are two conflicting reports. The records go on to state that the unit leader decided not to descend into the darkness right away, given the statement of soldier two. Soldier one protested that he had heard no sound and was confused by soldier two's report of what had happened. The leader was inclined to believe soldier two though, as he was allegedly displaying a fear that could not be a pretence or acting. Soldier two was said to be trembling in fear, wide-eyed and perspiring, and in genuine shock. The leader stated that he had seen true fear in man before battle over the years, and he was seeing it now."

"It was decided that the troops would escort the minerals to their final destination, which I believe was a large warehouse just east of Gloombest lake, then hastily assemble a larger and better equipped force before returning to Door 8 to carry out a fuller search for the missing soldier, Mooden. For whatever reason, that search party never materialised, and poor Mooden was left down there in the total darkness, alone and likely terrified, regardless of which soldier's report you believe."

"This story does not end there though, as there is some speculation that Mooden was 'found' a whole year later, down there in the tunnels, between Doors 14 and 15, quite a distance from Door 8. Three soldiers report coming across what they described as a ghost, a demon or a monster, depending on which of the three statements you read through. However, all three basically reported the same thing, which is something solid. The men had been guarding a small team of engineers who were paving a short section of the tunnel floor with cement and slabs. Even the most fearless engineers never declined an armed escort if working down in the tunnels, something I can reason with."

"The soldiers report feeling, rather than hearing, a shockwave wash over them. The soldiers were not the most well-read or lettered of men, so maybe lacked the descriptive forces that our venerable clerics possess, but they spoke of what seemed to be an outburst of dark shadow, one which their torches could do nothing against. The men all turned, instinctively, although all three reported that they wished they hadn't. A…some figure made of darkness floated down the tunnel towards the transfixed soldiers, slowly, as if moved by a non-existent wind. As the ghostly figure approached, the soldiers noted its glowing white eyes. Although the men told a very dubious interviewer that the eyes were more like holes to somewhere else."

"It wasn't so much that the shadow-being could see out, but that the men could see in. Into whatever was behind and within this shadow. The men spoke of glimpsing unspeakable things behind those two brilliant white portals, things beyond their vocabulary, and likely behind yours or mine. The men buried their faces in their hands and screwed their eyes shut.

One of the men confessed that he felt like removing his eyes, as seeing nothing was better than seeing what this being was showing him."

"The being presently spoke, although when pressed about the sound of the voice, all three men described, in their own words, the sense that the voice was coming from everywhere, and not directly from this shadow-being. The voice itself was from a nightmare, but the men remembered the words ad verbatim. Oddly, the men, interviewed separately, recounted the same harrowing sentences with no deviation."

"*I have your man-friend Mooden here with me. He looked into the darkness, and kept looking, eventually he saw through the darkness, and found what lay beyond. He came to me as no one came for him. He screamed for a long time until he moved beyond what you call 'madness' into the place he is at now, which I call 'the endless abyss'. A realm of pure nightmares. I have just shown you the mildest and most filtered taste of this realm, and you should be thankful that I chose to be so merciful. The thing that was Mooden is not afraid though, he is beyond fear. When he, or it, is truly ready, I will spit him back out into your narrow and fragile world. When that happens, you'd better hope that those invisible friends in the sky you call 'Gods' finally listen to your desperate screams for help, as no one else will save you.*"

"The men, who had been burying their hands in their faces all the while, eyes screwed shut, could sadly not block out the sound of the voice. Once the voice had stopped speaking though, the men finally raised their faces and slowly opened their eyes. The shadow-being had departed, leaving only the usual darkness of the tunnel. The men wisely chose not to remain down there a moment longer. They relayed to the engineers that they were leaving immediately, whether they were finished working or not. The engineers, who had been too far away from this traumatic meeting to even be aware of it, noticed the shaken state of the three soldiers and became infected by the fear. Engineers and soldiers alike made a hasty exit to the nearest exit door."

There was a pause as both Kurt and I pondered over this information, for it was a lot to take in. I could imagine a man getting left behind in the dark, screaming in terror, and eventually succumbing to insanity down there alone. But the spectre with portals for eyes?

"How much of their story do you believe, Robert? I mean, the soldier's report of the talking shadow telling them of Mooden's horrific fate?" I asked Robert.

Robert shrugged and shook his head, before responding: "Up until recently, I would say it sounds like the rantings of mad men. Maybe some gases linger down in the tunnels, which caused some manner of group hallucination. Maybe the men were already drunk and sleep deprived, and let their imaginations and terror get the better of them. Now though, I have seen our land invaded by a foreign army who are not men. I have seen our once blue and beautiful sky sicken to a permanent brownish fog. I have seen healthy trees and plants wither and die unusually fast for no good reason. Truthfully, I don't know what to believe anymore," Robert answered honestly.

I found myself agreeing with Robert's summary of the situation. To say that we were playing our game on uncertain terms was an understatement. This was unlike any war any of us had fought before. My troubled thoughts were interrupted by Kurt posing a question to Robert: "Robert, do you know what became of the three men who alleged to have witnessed this talking shadow?"

Ah, the three men in question were called Martin Stockford, Damon Law and Wolfgang Shule. They managed to give their reports shortly after the incident, the next day I believe. However, all three went downhill from then on. All three were discharged from the Halia army within a few weeks and had to look elsewhere for support. Stockford became a hopeless drunk, who could be seen staggering around low-class taverns ranting and raving about a talking ghost and two holes of evil. People paid his rantings little mind though and walked on by. Stockford eventually drunk himself into an early grave. I only hope he achieved some peace in death.

"Law's reaction to whatever happened in the tunnels was more extreme than Stockford's as he descended into full madness. He took the life of a young woman, a barmaid, one dark night around one month after his ordeal. As a result, he was taken into custody before being shipped out of Halia on a filthy prison barge. I have no idea what happened to Law after that. Shule simply packaged up what little he possessed before taking off into the remoteness of the Barren Mountains. Nothing was heard or seen of him after he left," Robert explained.

"How do you know so much, Robert? Aren't you a farmer?" I had to ask.

"Firstly, I have my contacts. I am not without eyes or ears. Secondly, I haven't always been a farmer," Robert explained, dropping me a sly smile.

It was the next day, during the early afternoon, when a final meeting was held. This time, the number of invitees was too large for the meeting to be conducted in the small and somewhat cosy office. This meeting was held in another larger side-chamber. I had a feeling that this was a meeting not for more information-gathering, but a meeting of action, a meeting to cement the next step.

Once again, Kurt chaired the meeting. Whilst Kurt was not the most senior man in the room, he was the most military-experienced and an expert in the ways of leading and protecting men in hazardous situations, be it direct combat or travelling through dangerous territory. I believe we all classed deep dark tunnels full of grizzly secrets as dangerous territory. So, it had been agreed between the higher-ups that Kurt would be in charge of the larger company's movements, at least until we reached Mirgot's Pass. Or hoped to reach Mirgot's Pass.

I sat with Vincent Harbrandt on my left and Bishop Edgeforth on my right. The good bishop was tending to his small flock of Apollatian followers—monks, clerics, novices, apothecaries and more assorted staff. They would be looking to their bishop for leadership, so it was important that he be aware of our plans going forward. Sitting opposite me was Lord Hartwright, who was representing around 12 soldiers and around the same in household staff, be they cooks, cleaners, medics, groundsmen or stableboys. The knowledgeable and well-connected Robert Howlett sat next to Lord Hartwright, hands folded in front of him. Also present around the larger table were two more lords and three military officers, none of whom I recognised or was introduced to during the meeting.

Kurt stood smartly at the head of the long table and cleared his throat loudly. Once he had everyone's attention, he commenced with his instructions in a regal voice, "My lords, Bishop Edgeforth, Captains and Sirs, I thank you for attending what I hope is our final meeting within this outpost. The last few days, if not longer, have been rough for all of us, and I apologise for any discomfort. I warn you though that the worst is most likely still to come. I am thankful that I still breathe Halian air, even if it is pretty stinky right now!"

This last sentence brought some much-needed humour to the assembled party, as a few chuckles were shared. Kurt continued on a more serious note: "As I believe most of you know, our final destination is the stronghold of Mirgot's Pass. I say the word 'stronghold', but I have little idea of what strength we will find at the pass, both in terms of men guarding the walls and the general state of repair. I have scouts travelling on the surface, relaying messages back to me. Unfortunately, I have heard nothing yet as far south as Mirgot's Pass. The Utreshians appear to be all over the land right now, which should come as no horrific surprise. It is only the wide and fast-flowing River Sovern which prevents them from reaching the pass."

"A direct route from here to Mirgot's Pass has been traced out, thanks to the expert knowledge of Robert Howlett. We will be travelling via the deep tunnels which lie underneath our feet, even here in the valley. We plan on entering the tunnels via Door 22, which lies some three miles from here. The route to Mirgot's Pass is between 15 and 16 miles, although please allow this as a rough number. Door 38 lies only half a mile from Mirgot's Pass."

"I could give you a time estimate, but it would be in poor faith. Truthfully, there is just no way of knowing how long it will take a larger group of people to travel those tunnels for a distance of at least 15 miles. This will be a journey of the like never seen before, so there is little to compare it to. All I ask is that we stick together, help each other, guard each other's backs, and keep pushing south no matter what. Yes, travelling on the surface would be easier, but it would be like walking into the jaws of a ravenous beast. We are too few in number for open battle, plus we have plenty of non-combatants who would be slaughtered like cattle."

"There are already numerous scouts of ours within the tunnels, checking the path ahead, so we will not be going in totally blind. Sadly, we simply do not have the resources to secure the whole 15-plus-mile route in advance. Time is not on our side here, my friends."

"I plan to travel in the vanguard of the group, with a dozen of my soldiers. Lord Hartwright, could you bring your men in line behind me? Then, Bishop Edgeforth, if you could lead your contingent behind that of Lord Hartwright? Then Lord Farnier, could you travel behind the good bishop? Lord Goodstock, if you would be so good as to move in behind Lord Farnier. Marcus, I would like you to take the rearguard alongside Officer Fullcowen and a dozen good soldiers. Officers Street and Lukas, you and your troops will guard the two flanks of the procession."

"I would remind you all that the order of the procession is by no means a reflection of importance or seniority, it is merely an order so that we are not just moving like a huge swarm of refugees. We are, and will remain, a serious military formation as much as possible. Each contingent will carry their baggage train behind them, and I will enforce that we take as little as possible for obvious reasons. Food, water, weapons and basic essentials only. If you can leave it here, I ask kindly that you do."

"The plan is that we leave here at dusk tomorrow and travel to Door 22 under the relative cover of darkness. We will assemble as quietly and orderly as we can in the valley itself before moving south. Get some rest and tomorrow make your final preparations. If I need to speak to any of you before then, I will send for you. Thank you, everyone, and good luck to us all."

With that final blessing, the meeting was effectively over. The attendees stood and slowly filed out of the room, none of them looking happy and some looking very bleak indeed. This was understandable as we had some rough and uncertain days ahead. This journey would not be easy for any of us, let alone what happened if and when we reached the final door out of the tunnels to Mirgot's Pass.

I spoke with my immediate group later that day, briefing them on the plan of action for dusk of the following day. They watched me with keen eyes and listened intently to my explanation and instructions. I reinforced the point about travelling light and leaving non-essentials behind, not that any of us had much of those in the first place given how we had arrived. We did however keep hold of the impromptu weapons we had taken from the ravaged village of Otter's Wall.

We had access to proper steel longswords by this stage, battle-axes and spears also, and most of us opted to equip ourselves with these. The impromptu weapons though carried a kind of allure to them, as if they were a kind of symbol, signifying the founding of our original band of eight companions. Mordak, although still recovering from his nasty leg wound and hobbling on a stick, refused to be parted from his trusty blacksmith's hammer. He admitted to me that he wanted to smash the skull of the next Utreshian he saw with that beast of a hammer. I patted him on his beefy shoulder and wished him luck.

I had posed the question of weapons training to Vincent a few days prior to the final meeting. He had been slightly stubborn at first and managed to find several excuses, but finally had acquiesced. Following Vincent's agreement, I had taken him through a total of six hours of training with the longsword and shield. Vincent had, of course, used a sword in games, so he was not a total novice with the weapon. But parrying against a fellow noble for the amusement of a crowd at a feast or event was very different to fighting tooth and nail against a furious opponent, or numerous opponents, who wanted to douse the floor with your guts.

Vincent had never fought for his life. Part of combat was controlling your fear, your adrenaline levels, your fatigue. That could not be taught, only learned the hard way through painful experience. Still, Vincent and I both felt more confident after that basic but perhaps lifesaving practice.

I spoke with my old friend Brother Abel about his feelings and thoughts on that last full day within the cavern outpost. I had always appreciated his wisdom and advice, and his opinion never failed to be important to me. We sat sharing a few drinks at one of the tables in the main cavern. Brother Abel seemed a little restless, as did we all, I guess.

"Marcus, I would rather we just leave and get this journey started, even if some of us may not see the end. It is the waiting that I find myself…hating…and that is not a word I use lightly. Whilst we sit down here doing little, our once fair land is being despoiled," expressed Brother Abel.

"I can only agree. I have heard many men say that the waiting is often the worst part, and they are not wrong. The wait is almost over though. Let's stay focused, stay together, and keep looking forward." I clasped the strong, weathered hands of Brother Abel and gave him a reassuring look as I spoke those words.

Shortly afterwards, sitting alone as the hall started to empty, I thought about the exact words I had said to Abel moments ago…'keep looking forward', which was really the same as not looking back. Once again, I found myself picturing my father standing tall against the bleak windy sky on Redcrag Mountain, as if nothing could move him. Once again, I heard my father's strong voice which I could hear even over the merciless gale, telling me to rise.

The next day, the final day, was a day of movement and action—people packing up belongings, soldiers checking and cleaning their equipment, the baggage trains themselves being double-checked to ensure that they were ready for travel, holy men delivering final blessings upon their followers, food being organised and packed into suitable containers. It had been decided that all but a few of the horses would be released before we departed, as there was no knowing how they would react down in the tunnels for what would be days on end. Better not risk terrorising them and having to deal with a maddened horse when there was so much else of concern. Sadly, no one amongst us could think of any suitable place to take them, so we had little choice but to just release them out in the open air to fend for themselves.

I had seen Kurt several times throughout the day, usually directing people or responding to the numerous final questions people needed answering before the journey began at dusk. He had looked flustered and stressed for the most part. I did not envy him at all, as I would not want his level of responsibility on top of everything else that was happening. Whilst I was envious of him, I did find myself admiring how he stepped up the task like a true leader, a true Halian pillar of strength.

Finally, as dusk began to settle and shadow engulfed the land, we found ourselves formed up outside in what we still hoped was a hidden section of Valmere Valley, more or less in the order detailed by Kurt the day before. I was heading up the rearguard as agreed, alongside this man I had only met the day before—Officer Joseph Fullcowen, a veteran of some 20 years' service from East Halia. I had introduced myself to Joseph following the final meeting, as we would be working directly together. He seemed a friendly enough fellow and brief pleasantries were exchanged.

I just hoped that Joseph would prove useful in combat if it came to that. It was possible, but rare, for a man to serve in the Halian forces for as long as twenty years and still never taste any real combat. If Joseph turned out to be such a man, then the leadership role would fall squarely on my shoulders. I had no choice in my battle brother though, orders were orders.

There was movement at the front as Kurt's vanguard began to move, and that was it, we were off into whatever darkness and danger lay ahead. I was nervous right then, not for the first or last time, and I felt no shame in admitting it. I knew that I was being watched though, and if I showed fear, it would become contagious. I was joint leader of the rearguard, so had to lead by example.

We moved as quietly as we could across the still land of Halia. Once my eyes adapted to the darkness, I spotted numerous shadowy figures crouching nearby but knew immediately that they were friends. Just Halian scouts keeping their eyes fixed for any incoming Utreshian troop movements. We saw some distant burning fires, and even heard some roars and screams come rolling across the barren fields, but these sounds indicated no immediate danger, so we kept pressing south.

The vanguard halted outside what looked to be an unremarkable-looking old oak tree, and the rest of the column followed suit in coming to a stop. After only a two- or three-minute wait, a rider appeared out of the night and carried a message from the vanguard that we had reached Door 22, the entrance to the tunnels. I allowed myself to exhale a minor sigh of relief that at least this first stretch of the journey had brought no trouble.

Next came the slow and arduous process of lowering the party down into the tunnels via the rope and pulley-operated platform system, bit by bit. Our whole company numbered around 80 people, as well as six baggage trains, so we at the rear of the group expected a long wait. We could not risk overloading the lift and potentially damaging it, so were careful with just how much we sent down with each descent. It was reported back that the first descent of 10 soldiers had reached the tunnel floor safely and nothing had broken, so we were looking at maybe 12 descents and ascents before the entire procession was down in the tunnels. This in itself wasn't a huge number, but we had to take time into consideration.

Each descent and ascent of the lift was slow, as the pulley system was operated by two men at either end of the lift shaft. So, I calculated in my head that the last of us could be waiting here in the dark, somewhat exposed and separated from the main body of the company, for what could be an hour, even if all went well. I did not express my concern to the men, however. They were simply ordered to wait and keep alert and in order.

We waited quietly whilst more and more of the company were lowered from one darkness into another. I could hear the sound of the platform being lowered and raised, the sound getting louder and quieter depending on the direction in which said platform was travelling.

I found my original estimate of an hour's uncomfortable waiting fairly accurate, for it was only a few minutes over an hour when I heard the lift rise, ready for the first of my two rearguard groups to descend. I found the sound both ominous and a relief in equal parts, which sounds odd, I can imagine. The rearguard totalled 14 men: Officer Fullcowen and I plus the twelve soldiers under our command. We were scheduled to descend in a group of seven and one of eight, as the pulley operator at the top had no reason to stay up there.

It was Officer Fullcowen who spotted the first sign of trouble behind us. "Do you see that burning torch being waved, out there in the darkness? That's one of our scouts, I'm sure."

I turned quickly to assess the situation, before also noticing the movement of the burning torch. The torch would wave side to side for two repetitions, before pointing into the darkness, roughly north-east. I followed the direction of the torch to see if I could spot anything. At first my eyes failed me and I only saw more shadow, but once I allowed my eyes to adjust slightly, I saw the darkness itself was moving and shifting. This vision was accompanied by the telltale clank of metal armour. Something not friendly was moving out there and the scout was alerting us to its presence.

"Men, form up, two lines of six soldiers. Officer Fullcowen and I will guard each end," I ordered out loud, hoping that Officer Fullcowen was not offended by being included in the order.

Any time for stealth was over, we had been spotted by the enemy and trying to become invisible would achieve nothing. The dozen soldiers obeyed the order, drawing their steel longswords and quickly forming into the two ranks.

As the moving darkness began to come closer and break up into the individual but numerous shapes of armoured enemy warriors, the sound of the lift getting closer reached my ears. In that instant, I knew that there were two choices on the table—stand and try and fight off this enemy body, or just turn and flee for the platform and try and descend before battle was joined. I opted for the latter.

"Men, about turn and make for the platform, now, but don't break rank. Officer Fullcowen and I will guard your retreat. We're not going to engage the enemy up here alone," I once again ordered, once again including my fellow officer in the order.

As instructed, the soldiers executed a hasty but ordered retreat into the upper deck of the lift shaft. Officer Fullcowen and I continued to face the incoming enemy and protect the backs of the retreating troops, our longswords held in a defensive position.

"All of you, onto the platform now! We will descend together," I yelled over my shoulder.

"Fourteen of us, Captain Kane? Can the platform bear our weight?" asked Officer Fullcowen in a somewhat desperate manner.

"We're going to have to try, we have no time for two descents. You there, operating the pulley, get on the platform! This is the last descent I'm afraid." This last part was delivered to the frightened-looking pulley operator. He would have had to have been in a coma not to understand our immediate predicament.

So the fifteen of us stood on the platform, with serious risk no matter whether we descended or stayed. There was danger down below and danger up here with us. I chose to go down. Maybe my subconscious mind was telling me that death from falling was somehow better than being carved up by a mob of bloodthirsty monsters.

"LOWER US NOW, QUICK AS YOU CAN!" I yelled down into the darkness, as the first of the Utreshian brutes was almost in sight of the door. I could see several more of his comrades over his broad armoured shoulders, teeth bared and eyes almost aglow in the rancid night.

Praise be, the lift started to descend with us fifteen bodies thankful for any momentum which would take us away from the incoming Utreshian blades. I was no coward and had already stood against a roomful of these brutes, but I did not want to throw all our lives away in a futile battle. If the Utreshians got control of the platform system, there was little to stop them lowering down a load of enemies to catch up with and mercilessly attack the rear of our company.

As the first of the brutes reached the edge of the upper platform, he lowered his hideous face to look down on our band of descending Halians, who returned his stare. The brute's face twisted in anger and he emitted a feral scream of rage. He had been so close to his prey and had let them wriggle away. The brute's scream continued, as he chose not to simply let us go so easily but continue the chase.

By now, we were a good 12 feet down the shaft, but this was apparently nothing to the angry brute, who launched himself into the air, before flying down to land nosily on the platform. The lone Utreshian stood little chance, as three armed soldiers moved in hacking and slicing before the brute had even recovered from his jarring impact. The brute had not lost his ugly cleaver on impact but was too slow to muster any kind of defence against three fast-moving longswords. After a few hurried blocks and parries, the brute was down and unmoving.

We will never know if the platform could have carried the fifteen of us safely to the bottom of the shaft, for the impact of a raging 18-stone body hitting the already strained platform at speed pushed the whole system over the edge. As soon as the focus of the fight was over and the brute silenced, we heard the awful sound of ropes coming apart and wood tearing. The once reasonably smooth descent of the platform became jagged and stop-start. All we passengers could do was keep still and balance ourselves, ready for any fall. No one dared move, blink or even breathe. The platform seemed to drop into free-fall for another 10 feet, before stopping momentarily, knocking several men to their knees. Then, all I remember was the platform totally giving way and flying down into nothingness.

In my dream, I was running, running from something truly terrifying. I was hurtling across the open area below Mirgot's Pass, as if running for the safety of the thick and towering walls. My lungs were burning, my eyesight was hazy, as if on the edge of absolute exhaustion. I turned my head to see the subject of my fear, already knowing that it was a mistake. For that huge giant I had seen back in Carnagon Castle was charging towards me, his feral eyes glowing in his gigantic skull. He was even larger than I remembered, now over 8 feet in height and wider than any war horse I had seen. His raging footsteps shook the very ground around us, and the shaking only got worse as he closed the distance.

I knew that I would not reach the pass in time. I turned at the last moment to see the giant right above me, ready to finish it all. He opened his mouth in a huge roar, displaying two huge rows of flesh-tearing fangs.

Fortunately, my harrowing nightmare was interrupted as I found myself slowly coming back into the land of the living. I sat up carefully, eyes still screwed shut and my hand massaging what felt like a sore head. I detected a presence nearby and turned to see Brother Abel looking at me with relief.

"Marcus, you gave us quite a scare. It's good that you are back with us," Brother Abel spoke quietly.

"What…what happened? I remember that Utreshian jumping down onto the platform and we killed him. Then…nothing," I said groggily.

"Ah, we were reorganising ourselves down in the tunnels when we heard the sounds of a scuffle coming from the platform. We heard the clash of steel alongside some shouting. Then some seconds later, a horrific crashing sound came from the bottom of the lift shaft. Those nearby, of which I was one, rushed to the scene to see what had happened. We found the platform in near splinters, with a huge load of soldiers, more than the lift could carry, lying in varying states of injury.

"Now, take solace in the fact that none of you are dead and none will die from the accident. You only suffered a mild concussion, with a minor cut on your forehead. Nothing that you haven't taken from a battle a hundred times, I imagine. There are a few broken bones shared amongst the group, but nothing life-threatening," Brother Abel explained helpfully.

It was all starting to come back to me. The Utreshian war party rushing towards Door 22. The lowering of the overburdened platform. The force of the falling Utreshian causing the overstrained pulley system to give way.

"The Utreshians. Did any more follow us down?" I asked Abel, more eagerly now.

"No more of them jumped down, no. We did look up to the surface but couldn't really see anything in the darkness. The decision was made to fire the whole lift shaft to dissuade the enemy from following us down, for a while at least. So, the good news is that the enemy cannot easily get down into the tunnels from Door 22. The bad news, as if we needed anymore, is a reverse of the good news; we cannot now leave via Door 22 even if we wanted to, as there is no longer a lift platform."

"Also, the Utreshians now know that a number of their enemy are travelling underground, although I pray that they do not know anything further about the tunnel system. My mind struggles to cope with what would happen if they something found another door ahead of us, and behind, and closed us off down here," Brother Abel responded.

That last possibility didn't bear thinking about. Although, we would be fools not to be ready for anything. We had to expect the unexpected.

Before long, I was up and walking again and leading the rearguard alongside Officer Fullcowen. Joseph Fullcowen had damaged his leg during the fall, and so had been gifted the use of a horse as the injury troubled his walking too much. Nine of the original twelve soldiers who had been involved in the fall still walked under their own steam, whilst the other three who had taken more serious injuries were gratefully transported on top of the baggage train.

We fell into a steady pace for those first few days of walking south from Door 22. We would walk for several miles, before allowing the whole party to rest a little. We were determined not to split the company but continue to travel as one long connected body of soldiers, people and supplies. There were no official mealtimes; different contingents within the group just refreshed themselves as and when. We had been advised by Kurt that we could speak quietly amongst ourselves but take care to avoid making too much noise.

We had little idea of what may be lurking in these tunnels and did not want to draw unwanted attention from anything that may be prowling in the dark. Robert's earlier stories about the alleged wolf creatures, giant rats, monstrous spiders and talking shadows had sounded like fantasy when we heard them in the relative safety of the outpost study. However down there in those dark tunnels, those tales came back to me with an all too sobering sense of reality. I would not be laughing if I encountered any of those creatures.

Around 6 miles into the tunnel journey though, those fears materialised, as the tunnel residents gave us a belated welcome reception. One that we would have been all too happy not to attend.

The first sign of trouble was when the company slowly came to an untimely halt. Even from my position in the vanguard, I could hear the sound of raised voices but did not have the advantage of a line of sight, so could not see what was happening. Before long, an outrider clad in tough leather armour and a metal helmet pulled up beside me and addressed both Captain Fullcowen and I. A large brown destrier neighed nervously from under the rider, as if detecting the rising panic.

"Captains. Captain Winters has sent me to relay a message. There is an incoming party of potential hostiles. So far, they have not responded to any calls to identify themselves. They appear to be armed and are showing signs of aggression. Captain Winters asks that you stay vigilant and watch for any threat from the rear."

I was just about to thank the man and agree to Kurt's instructions, when the sudden and hair-raising sound of snarling could be heard from the shadows behind us. Every man in the vanguard turned to see what creature had made the snarling. I could see nothing at first in the inky darkness, no matter how hard I tried to focus. But then several sets of shining eyes seemed to come into view, some of which were alarmingly far off the tunnel ground, as if belonging to hideously tall beings.

I turned to the outrider with my own instructions, "Return to Captain Winters and warn him that the vanguard could be under attack any moment now as well. We have a group of hostiles closing in."

The outrider nodded and turned his destrier before disappearing back up towards the head of the column. By now, several of the spear-carrying troops guarding the flank of the column were moving towards the rearguard's location, ready to provide combat support if necessary. The sounds of animalistic snarling only increased as more throats added to the din. The creatures were almost within range of the glow of our torches. It was as if they were gathering themselves and testing our strength from the shadows before committing to an all-out attack. So, whatever these things were, they were not totally mindless, I remember thinking as our party stood ready with hands on sword hilts.

"Stay back. Come no further," I shouted boldly into the darkness at the gathering line of creatures.

I could see that most were roughly man-sized and may once have been men who looked very much like us. The taller creatures amongst them stood well over seven feet and seemed distorted and twisted. They looked slightly emaciated, but still showed stringy muscle and did not look weak. They were clad in filthy-looking rags, and some wore what looked to be scavenged armour, whilst brandishing primitive weapons made of sticks and stones.

The shadowy horde chose to ignore my demand, as I feared they would. The twenty-strong horde then came fully into the torchlight, teeth bared and eyes aglow with hatred and madness.

"Men, prepare for battle, ready your swords!" I ordered my rearguard.

The men responded hastily, pulling their steel longswords from their scabbards and bracing themselves for combat. The chorus made by so many swords being drawn at once was music to my ears, even given the present situation. My order was not a moment too soon, as the front line of the horde surged forward, accompanying their rush with their own chorus of terrifying howls.

The two lines of combatants met, as men and creature began exchanging frantic blows. Whilst strength of numbers was on our opponent's side, everything else was on our side. We possessed the superior armour and weaponry and, it seems, training. I joined the melee, hacking and slashing remorselessly into the pack of enemies. Within minutes, numerous dead creatures littered the floor of the tunnel in expanding pools of blood. I could not help but notice that even in the poor light, their blood looked remarkably similar to ours, adding weight to my theory that these creatures had been men at some stage, before some awful fate twisted them into some new monstrous form.

Sadly, I spotted some of my Halian brethren lying still alongside the corpses of those they had just sent to the next life. One poor fellow's entire face seemed to have been caved in with a well-placed axe strike, whilst another Halian had been ripped open at the neck. I had little time to ponder their fates though, as more of the fiends assailed me from both left, front and right. Our rearguard fought shoulder to shoulder, valiantly and without pause, until the entire attacking group had been dealt with. It was only then we allowed ourselves to catch our breath and rest our burning limbs.

My eyes met with those of Officer Fullcowen, whose bloodied sword told of the carnage he had just wrought. He was bent over with his hands on his knees and his head turned towards me, breathing heavily. "What were those things, Captain Kane? They looked almost like men."

I automatically looked back at the gory littering of enemy bodies on the tunnel ground, as if to get a better picture of what they were before answering Fullcowen, when my eyes passed further into the shadows. I found my throat getting dry and my heart rate increasing even further, as I spotted more sets of eyes out there in the darkness. Then it hit me, we had dealt with only the first wave of these creatures. That twenty-strong attack had merely been a test.

"Men, it isn't over, I'm afraid, look there. Prepare yourselves again!" I ordered, indicating where the fighting men should be focusing their gaze.

The fighting men, despite their fatigue and the knowledge that they were outnumbered, once again stood to the mark with their weapons ready. They were of true Halian stock and I swelled with pride to be commanding them. There were now only six of our original twelve rearguard troops standing alongside me in that tunnel; on top of the few who had just been killed, several were recovering from injuries sustained in the fall and were not combat-ready.

As a much larger body of the creatures edged closer and closer, at least thirty of the swine, I yelled back over my shoulder for backup. I was encouraged to see six or seven spear-wielding guardsmen come running eagerly to reinforce our dwindling force. I tried not to even think about the 'numbers' problem, in that once a Halian fighting man was out of the game, it wasn't like he could be replaced down here. Whereas these creatures could be nigh on limitless. Just how many enemies would we find in these miles and miles of dark and lost tunnels? Hundreds? Thousands? We could not afford to engage in many more open battles like this.

However, right then, we had no choice. We could not run. It was stand and fight, and if we all died, I just hoped that I left this world in what the bards might call a 'warrior's death'!

Once again, we braced ourselves shoulder to shoulder and let the enemy come to us. Once again, the enemy surged forward, and the second phase of the battle commenced. I dropped back into my rhythm of blocking, parrying, hacking and slashing whilst trying to protect the soldiers on my left and right. I felt a burst of relief every time another fiend dropped under my sword, and before long, there was an impressive pile of corpses at my feet.

Other Halians along the line were not faring so well though, as I heard several mortal screams coming from our side of the battle line. Screams that indicated that whilst the enemy numbers were depleting, so were ours. I took another quick check during a slight break in combat to scan our lines, both left and right of my position. We were down to maybe seven fighting men, standing against some twenty or more of the fiends.

Our soldiers were already fatigued, and some were gritting their teeth against injuries the enemy blades had inflicted. I tried to keep up hope but felt that it was a losing battle and that a warrior's death was the best I could hope for. I hoped that the rest of the company would be able to continue their mission and make it to relative safety. I felt that the cold hand of the reaper was about to finally grab my shoulder and take me off.

I was entertaining what I was almost sure were my final thoughts when I heard an almighty battle cry from behind me.

I turned in wonder to see who could be coming to our aid. I felt my hope soar as I saw a strong wedge of soldiers, led by a charging and howling Mordak, who was wielding his trusty blacksmith's hammer. Even in the relative darkness of the tunnel, I could see that Mordak had adapted the hammer somehow, made it stronger.

Flanking Mordak in the wedge were my comrades from the original brotherhood—young Simon Fester brandishing his shining longsword, Gustav racing in with round shield and battleaxe at the ready, Peter also bracing a longsword and eager to make up for any previous acts of cowardice, and finally I spotted Lord Vincent Harbrandt himself, sword in hand and hungry for combat. Behind this immediate wedge of 5 came three more Halian troops to make a total of eight.

Whilst the enemy still outnumbered us even with our gallant reinforcements, the pure strength of the reinforcements knocked any real wind out of the fiends. Mordak bowled into the crush of enemies like a raging bull, using his large frame and speed to break open their ranks. Watching the spectacle was like watching a fierce tidal wave wash away all in its path. As several of the enemies were knocked to the ground, Mordak continued to lay about him with the hammer, brutally crushing skulls and mangling limbs.

The rest of the comrades followed in behind their hulking frontman, adding their own swinging blades or and axes to the carnage. Our surviving rearguard took this opportunity to press on with a renewed attack, hacking and slashing with vigour at the startled fiends, who were more hunters and predators than any kind of warrior.

Within a space of minutes, the battle had ended with us as the victors. A field of enemy bodies and a gore-slicked ground spoke of our bloody triumph, minor as it was. As the Halians still standing checked the wounded and finished off any still-moving fiends, I walked over to greet our leading saviour, Mordak.

"Well met, my friend. I cannot thank you enough for your timely intervention. Lord knows what would have happened had you not arrived when you did," I acknowledged.

"Think nothing of it, Captain. We would have come sooner, but there was trouble up at the front as well. As soon as that was handled, we raced back here to see how you were faring," Mordak confirmed, his big face blood-slicked and haunting in the torchlight.

"Did you take many losses up there?" I asked, before hesitantly asking a more direct question: "Does Captain Winters still stand?"

"Aye, Captain Winters is unhurt, although we lost several good troops to the fiends. Fiends who looked like this," Mordak promptly responded, pointing to a nearby lifeless body of a sinewy humanoid who had accosted us.

"This was likely as far as these beasts go in terms of battle manoeuvres. Anyway, all this blood and carnage will only alert more of whatever dwells in these tunnels. We need to be moving onwards. We cannot afford any more of these skirmishes if we want to reach Mirgot's in one piece," I advised.

So, the remnants of the company continued to progress southwards through the tunnels, much as before, only more alert and anxious given our depleted strength. We continued mile after mile, stopping to rest when we needed to and holding meetings whenever the need arose. Fortunately, we encountered no tunnel blockages which demanded a turnaround, although in some stretches the baggage carts had needed to be almost wrestled over loose rubble.

In other parts, we found ourselves almost ankle-deep in foul water which had pooled on the tunnel floor. Robert Howlett was invaluable as the map reader, always prompt to field questions about our route and how we were faring. If Robert had any doubts, he did not share them. Robert must have been aware that the company was essentially depending on him to guide them through the darkness to the light. If he expressed doubts, then this would cascade throughout the party. If Robert were to tell them that they were totally lost and throw his maps on the ground in despair, then it would all be over.

The company was fearful and anxious enough as it was, with the combination of oppressive darkness and the never-ending fear of what could be lurking in the shadows for them. The company's military strength was already under half of what it had been prior to that vicious attack, and it would not be getting any stronger.

We were around five miles from that final door to Mirgot's Pass when the company slowly halted. I was on the verge of ordering a nearby outrider to gallop up to the vanguard and ask what the delay was, when what I can only describe as a pulse of energy flowed down the tunnel. I was certain that everyone else felt it too.

I looked around to witness shocked and perplexed faces. The pulse had not caused any damage or pain as such, it just seemed more of an alert. My mind went back to that story we had been told by the knowledgeable Mr Howlett himself about the horrific fate of one Teryn Mooden. I had found that story hard to fathom then, but down there in the tunnel, after having felt that unexplainable pulse of energy, I was not so sure that it was the fiction many had concluded it to be.

I swiftly ran up to the outrider and somewhat directly commandeered the use of his horse. I wasted no time in galloping up to the head of our group, leaving a startled Officer Fullcowen, who had survived the battle of the fiends, in charge of the rearguard.

As I reached the vanguard, I noticed that they were all still and unspeaking. I was about to ask for an update, but it did not take long for me to see what they were seeing. I felt what I called 'reality' come apart, as I saw with my own eyes the moving 'shadow' that the hapless soldiers had reported seeing all those years ago. I was rendered speechless, motionless and even witless for a terrible few moments, until I found myself stammering out loud to the group: "Don't…don't look in…into its eyes. Just…just don't look."

I immediately looked at the ground and was grateful that others around me seemed to have also lowered their heads to focus on anything other than those terrible eyes. I felt the shadow coming and was bracing myself for the sound of its voice. The voice which had been described as coming from everywhere and sounding like that from a nightmare. I would find out myself what it sounded like soon enough, I figured.

"Do not be alarmed, men of Halia. I am not here as your enemy, not currently at least. You can look if you wish. It will be harrowing, I warn you, however I have closed access to the void, so you will at least retain your minds."

Despite these words of mild consolation, most men's heads continued to look downwards, clearly not convinced by the shadow's introduction. I found my head raising, almost as if controlled by an outside force. I found my eyes slowly opening, apparently whether I wanted them to or not.

It was then that I finally laid eyes upon this shadow. It was harrowing, yes, but hadn't this whole journey been harrowing? I could see no white portals to madness and just prayed that they would not suddenly open and wipe away my sanity on one fell swoop. But for some bizarre reason, I found myself believing that this shadow was not here to harm us. The shadow spoke again, its voice harsh upon the ears and terrible, but also bearable: "I have here the man-thing that was Mooden. He has still retained some of his former self and memories. He told me that he recognises one of you, a Kurt Winters. He wishes to speak to this Winters right now. This meeting will go ahead regardless of whether Winters wishes it or not."

It was then that all eyes focused on Winters, before the already strange events moved onto the next barely believable stage. Kurt's head jerked upright, to stare directly at the shadow. His eyes bulged open in shock. His mouth hung agape, as if gulping in vast amounts of air. Then, in front of our incredulous eyes, Kurt Winter's whole body was raised into the air, as if on an invisible rope. This freakish levitation stopped at around 10 feet into the air, shortly before Kurt was due to bash his head against the hard rock of the tunnel roof.

We could only watch in awe as Kurt's body hung there in space for some minutes on end, quite motionless. No one tried to drag him back down or accost the mysterious shadow. Maybe like me, they knew that whatever was happening was out of our control and to intervene would only make things worse. There was some communication happening between this shadow, or maybe Mooden himself, and Kurt, which was taking place at a level beyond our understanding.

When Kurt began descending, it was thankfully slow and gentle. Kurt's body was not just dropped like a sack to potentially injure himself. As he neared the ground, several nearby men supported his body and lay him down safely on the tunnel ground. His eyes were closed at this stage, but he still appeared to be breathing. Men closed in to get a better look, and finally questions started to be voiced nervously in the gloomy tunnel:

"Is he still alive?"

"Should we try and wake him?"

"What was that shadow?"

"What the heck just happened?"

"What made him float in the air?"

"Where is that sha—"

This last question was cut off mid-sentence, as Kurt's eyes suddenly jerked open in shock and he began gasping. Men moved back to give him some space, as he slowly sat up and started rubbing the bridge of his nose as if clearing a bad dream. No one spoke, all waiting for Kurt to say something. Shortly, Kurt started speaking, and it was the most incredible tale any of us had ever heard.

"I remember standing there in the tunnel and watching that shadow approach with everyone else. I remember the shadow talking and telling us not to be alarmed. I was trying not to look, like Marcus told us not to. I then remember hearing that terrible voice speak my own name. Then, I went somewhere else."

"I found myself in what I can only describe as nothingness. I felt like I was floating in a void, with no sound, or sight, or anything. There was just…nothing anywhere. It was beyond any kind of terrifying and I feared I would simply die from this terror. Before this happened, thankfully, I saw a figure which appeared to be made of light drifting towards me. I focused with all I had on this approaching island of light. It was all I had to stop myself from totally coming apart."

"The figure looked essentially like a man, but it was as if the human was trapped behind several layers of light. Words fail me to describe what I saw, but that is the closest I can get. The being of light began to speak in a voice mercifully more bearable than that hideous shadow-being in the tunnel. The being identified itself as what used to be the Halian solider, Teryn Mooden. I was told that Mooden's soul and spirit still existed but was part of a greater being now. I asked where I was and why I was alone in this void, fearing the answer, but less terrified than I had been moments earlier."

"The being that was Mooden told me that I was in a place called 'the endless abyss', and I knew that I had heard those words before, somewhere. The being went on to the say that my mind was being shielded from the horrors around me, as to so much as glimpse such horrors would have meant my immediate death. That explained the apparent nothingness. Even in that state, I recall being grateful that such a kindness was shown, if you can even call it that. The being then answered my second question about being alone in the void."

"It was then that the voice changed slightly, and I could hear what seemed to be Mooden himself speaking. His voice seemed to be coming from miles away, as if heard down a long tunnel. I could still make out what he was saying though. Mooden, what was left of him, told me that I had been chosen for this meeting, as I was the one who could give Mooden's spirit what he wanted, which was release and the chance to finally pass on. Mooden was trapped in the abyss, and only one thing could free him. The majority of you men do not know the story of Teryn Mooden's fate; however, to be brief, he was a soldier who was essentially abandoned down in the tunnels and left to rot several years ago. No rescue mission was ever executed."

"Mooden told me that it was no accident he was left in the tunnel and no search party was ever going to be sent. Mooden told me that he had been offered willingly as a sacrifice by his immediate commander. A commander who still lives to this day and goes by the name of Sir Henry D'Arten. This D'Arten had apparently made some ghoulish blood pact with the demon who presides over the endless abyss. The demon had somehow infiltrated D'Arten's dreams to offer and finally seal the deal. The demon contacted D'Arten as it could sense D'Arten's wicked nature and greed."

"Once Mooden was given up to the demon, D'Arten would be gifted with extended life and vitality and be free from disease and ailment. I asked why it was me specifically who had been chosen for this task. Mooden then told me something I had not seen coming. He told me that I am of the same blood as Henry D'Arten. He is, in fact, my half-brother of whom I had no knowledge. I have been tasked with finding and slaying Sir Henry D'Arten, my half-brother I never knew. Mooden informed me that once D'Arten lies dead, his spirit will finally be released from its prison."

"Upon hearing this, my mind finally moved towards our current situation. I agreed to go ahead with my task, Gods help me. However, I told Mooden about the Utreshian invasion, and how we were facing fearful odds against these foreign invaders. I pushed my luck and reminded Mooden that he was once a Halian soldier, tasked with defending this land. I asked if Mooden could help us at all, in any way, before he was released."

"Mooden was silent for a moment, and then I could hear a bizarre and deeply unnerving babble of voices coming from seemingly everywhere at once. I knew that Mooden was conversing with some other power or powers, although any conversation was well beyond my comprehension. Then there was silence again, before Mooden spoke to me. He agreed to help us in our plight. I was instructed to slay D'Arten right at the moment of our greatest peril. If I do that, then the being that was Mooden will be released and unleashed upon our enemies."

There was some silence after Kurt stopped speaking. Kurt then simply stared ahead into the gloomy tunnel, taking time to regain himself, I can imagine. I was struggling to process what I had just heard and doubted that anyone in the party was much different. I had so many questions I didn't know where to start. However, I had to ask something: "Does anyone know this Henry D'Arten, or where we might find him?"

My question was met with blank stares and shrugs, as I had predicted.

"Let's just keep pressing on to Mirgot's Pass. I'm pretty sure we aren't going to find D'Arten walking around down here," came the voice of good Brother Abel.

"Yes, that sounds like a good idea. I don't want to be in this tunnel a moment longer than necessary," came the agreement of poor Kurt, who was being helped shakily to his feet.

I could feel the general spirit of the group rise the nearer we got to Mirgot's Pass. 5 miles, 4 miles, 3 miles, 2 and a half miles, then 2 miles…Finally, our guide Robert told us that only a quarter of a mile separated us from that final door out to Mirgot's Pass and daylight, even if it was a poor daylight. I should have known that that final stretch was not going to be an easy stroll.

I was walking alongside my battle brother, Officer Fullcowen, speculating on what we might expect to find at Mirgot's Pass. I was hoping to find something more than a shell, as were we all, I can imagine. Our men and supplies alone would not be enough to offer much of a defence against a serious assaulting force.

I was in the midst of telling Fullcowen how high the walls were, when a rearguard scout alerted us to another nearby body of intruders. Both Fullcowen and I stared back into the gloom, and yes, the scout's sharp eyes were not seeing things that weren't there. I spotted the gathering horde and felt my heart sink as I knew the shape and manner of Utreshians. It was only a matter of time before they managed to find another way into the tunnels. We should have counted ourselves lucky that it took as long as it did.

"Rider, ride to the vanguard and warm them that Utreshian forces approach! We need to move at double pace," I called over to the nearby messenger, using a hushed yet clear voice.

The outrider nodded briskly before spurring his trusty horse off to the front of the company. I advised Fullcowen that we should just continue walking onwards and not try and offer resistance here. I glanced over my shoulder again and was not surprised to see that the Utreshian party was getting closer. I could begin to make out numbers in the dark, and almost wished that I couldn't. This was a serious force approaching, large enough to run right over us should it come to direct battle. No, we could not afford to close with the enemy down here.

I breathed a minor sigh of relief when the group in front us started to pick up the pace. I was inspired that Kurt had trusted my judgement enough to act upon it. Still, we would not be able to outrun the Utreshians even at this increased speed. An idea then came to me. Amongst the baggage train could be found plenty of cooking oil and alcohol, as well as other liquids that could be set alight. If we could douse the tunnel ground with such liquids and make a fire, it would at least act as an obstacle to our ruthless pursuers. I wasted no time in setting this plan in motion.

I, along with several other men, dashed forward to the cook's baggage train. I quickly explained my idea to the worried-looking head cook, who nodded his approval eagerly before indicating where such liquids could be found. It was unlikely that he had a better idea. Plus that oil would be no good to anyone if we all died down in that tunnel.

Shortly, several barrels of cooking oil were shouldered or dragged to the back of the company. I ordered the barrels to be broken open and the contents dashed across the tunnel. As this was going ahead, it seemed that the Utreshians became wise to our plan. They had no intention of losing their prey yet again, so made their move. The front line of the Utreshians, who were by then barely 50 feet away, broke into an all-out charge.

"Light the oil now!" I yelled at a terrified-looking soldier holding a lit torch.

The torch left the man's hand and seemed to move in slow motion through the air. I could not even contemplate what would happen if the oil did not light. I held my breath and watched with wide eyes as the torch finally hit the oil. For a horrifying moment, nothing happened and I felt death close in upon me, upon us. But then, praise be, the oil decided to react, throwing up a beautiful flare of orange light down there in the darkness. The flame quickly spread across the small sea of oil, lighting up both our faces and the hideous faces of the incoming enemy horde.

The enemy stopped short of the fierce wall of flame, shielding their faces from the worst of the heat. I knew that it would not hold them for long. Luckily, my comrade Kurt Winters was only 20 feet behind me, staring in awe at the sea of fire and the furious horde trying to cross it.

"Kurt, we need to run. We need to grab whatever we can carry and run!" I yelled out loud, barely stopping to consider that I was giving my commanding officer an order.

Kurt did not reprimand me, only nodded and took up agreeance. "Everyone, just leave the baggage train. Grab whatever you can in your hands and run for the door. There is no time," Kurt ordered, running back to the head of the company as he bellowed out his commands.

All along the company line, people took heed and did as they were told. I could see all the Halians, from cooks, to monks, to soldiers, to lords, grabbing their essentials and running south towards that final door. I had already slung my personal backpack over my shoulders and was making sure that my troops were in front of me and moving. I would have been no real leader if I had simply fled for my life and left everyone to their own fates.

So, we all ran for that door; legs pumping, breath harsh and cutting in our throats, lungs burning, bodies breaking out in sweat, teeth gritted against the fear and the pain. If anyone dropped anything, they were most likely to just leave it for the horde. I ran past several heavy-looking cases and sacks that the original bearer clearly didn't feel the need to die for.

I dared not risk a look over my shoulder at our pursuers. I was only looking forward. I just prayed that I would not feel the cold kiss of an Utreshian cleaver across the back of my neck. I could not shut out the sound of their screams though. They sounded like they had broken through the flames already.

I took strength in the fact that the vanguard had reached and managed to open that final door out of that stinking chasm of darkness and misery. I could see a small patch of daylight just ahead of me, which grew as I pushed myself for those last few metres. By this stage, the majority of the company had exited the confines of the tunnel. It was just myself and several of my troops sprinting ahead of me.

"Run Marcus, RUN!" Kurt screamed at me from the doorway.

I did not need to turn to know that the first of the Utreshians was barely a few feet behind me. I could hear his pounding steps and feel his huge form rushing in behind me. I could also feel my own energy ebbing and my body just giving in. The doorway seemed so far away and I lost hope that I would reach it. That is, until something incredible happened. I had never really been a religious man before that moment and never favoured any God, but from somewhere I was given a final burst of energy, strength and hope I never knew was in me.

I ran faster than I could have thought possible and for a few glorious moments almost felt like I could fly. As soon as I blasted through the final door into the murky daylight, Kurt and several others shut the hefty door in the faces of the Utreshians. Other soldiers took up spears and held the enemy at bay as the door was secured, jabbing viciously at any snarling faces or grabbing hands that tried to escape the tunnel. The door itself was something else—4 inches of hardened wood reinforced with strips of iron and steel. A heavy block was placed across the door, further barring exit to the thrashing and furious Utreshians behind the door.

"It won't hold them forever. I'll…have a load of stones and…rubble piled up in front of the door…just to buy us as much time…as possible," panted Kurt, still recovering from the adrenaline-filled sprint.

For now, at least, we were somewhat safe, and out of that dark and oppressive network. I turned my head to the sky, and for the first time in a while, laughed out in joy.

Mirgot's Pass itself was only around 100 feet from the final door we had recently emerged from. I had to crane my neck slightly to take it all in. I had never actually seen the place before and the walls were higher than I had expected. Sentries were visible on the wall; little heads observing us from on high. So at least we knew that Mirgot's had not been lying desolate. Whilst the survivors were regaining their breath and doing an inventory of their equipment, our leader Kurt Winters approached the wall before coming to a stop some 30 feet away. Kurt raised his head and looked up at the guards on the wall before uttering an introduction.

"I am Captain Kurt Winters, formerly of Barford Castle, which has now been lost to the enemy. I am the military commander of this contingent of Halians. I desire to speak to your commander," bellowed Kurt into the sky.

By now, the company had mostly paused to witness this exchange and to see how the Mirgot defenders would react. Luckily, they did not have to wait long for a response, as the Mirgot commander in question identified himself promptly.

"I am Major Simon De'Beresford. This outpost is under my command. How may I be of service?" came the commander's response, also shouted loudly so that all could hear.

"I would ask that you open your gates and allow us access, without delay. You must have heard about the approaching enemy forces. We need protection," Kurt responded.

There was then a brief conferring on the ramparts between De'Beresford and some of the other troops. We all waited in silence, eager for a positive response. However, we were to be disappointed in this aspect. For the Major's response was negative, and the very last thing we needed to hear.

"I am truly sorry, Captain Winters, but we cannot allow your party entry. You will have to seek shelter elsewhere. The safety of Farchester is our primary concern. We will not jeopardise it."

Kurt was about to respond to this refusal, when suddenly Lord Vincent Harbrandt himself was at Kurt's shoulder. He stood tall and upright, shoulders back. I was gladdened, inspired even, that he had managed to once again take up the role of a lord despite all he had been through.

"Major De'Beresford. I have no doubt you recognise me. However, I will remind you. I am Lord Vincent Harbrandt, Keeper of the Lafroide Valley. I sent troops to your aid only 18 months ago when you were in dire need, saving not only your life but those of your men. With our group is Lord Hartwright, the same lord who gifted your family grants of land in Brave's Reach."

"Additionally, if you look closely at our group, you will also spot Bishop Edgeforth, who I know gave you solace and hope during some very dark times. You think that we are a threat, Major De'Beresford? We have travelled miles through those wretched tunnels back there and lost many good men, just to get here. We are tired, hungry and at our wits end. You are our last hope, Major. When the enemy get here, and they will, you will need every pair of hands you can get to defend these walls."

Once again, there was a minor conference on the ramparts. Words which were exchanged beyond our hearing. Shortly, the Major delivered his response, which was more positive than the first, but still guarded, "It is good to see you again, Lord Harbrandt. I can assure you that I have never and will never forget what you did for us out at Bayland's Drift. I will allow you access to Mirgot's Pass; however, please tread carefully. Whilst I know you and some of the more noble members of your retinue, there are many who are strangers to me."

Kurt turned to face Lord Harbrandt, before thanking him profusely for his help. I can imagine we were thankful down to the last man. Vincent's impassioned speech had just saved our lives, if only for a while.

Once the defenders had opened the sturdy double doors to the pass, we began the slow progress of moving both ourselves and the little equipment we still carried inside the building. We could not afford to rest immediately though as there were tasks to attend to. We needed to organise sleeping arrangements, duty rosters, check on the food situation for all the hungry mouths, as well as get a full update from Major De'Beresford. Fortunately, there was plenty of space inside for all of our people. The pass was a huge construct and had only been lightly manned when we arrived at the walls. The interior decoration was sparse with its bare floorboards, naked stone walls and basic furniture. It was a place built for design and purpose, not style. That suited me fine.

I will never forget the moment that I ascended one of the flights of stone steps to emerge on the highest rampart of the pass. The view over the Golden City of Farchester was breathtaking. I had seen Farchester before, but never like that. *So that city is what I might die defending*, I remembered thinking to myself.

I turned and looked the other way, north, over the desolate wasteland. The view was as unforgettable as that of Farchester, just in a totally different way. From here, I could see the full devastation and destruction wrought by the Utreshian invasion. The smoke from burning towns, villages and castles could still be seen drifting up into the sky. Only the strongest and oldest trees still stood, and even those looked diseased and wilting.

I let my eyes travel slightly further north, to the wide River Sovern, the only obstacle the Utreshians faced before reaching Mirgot's Pass. I could just about spot the large bodies of men, or beings, working on the other side of the river. There seemed to be a lot of construction work going on. The Utreshians would be building makeshift bridges as a means to cross the river. The existing bridges had all been raised by the defenders of Mirgot's Pass on the approach of the invaders. This unfortunately cut off the escape south for friends as well as foes, but the safety of Farchester had to come first.

It was during my sightseeing from the high walls that Lord Harbrandt approached me, before commenting on the remarkable view, "It feels like you can see the whole world from up here. Shame that we weren't admiring the view north some three weeks ago before the Utreshians made their amendments to the landscape."

"Vincent, I cannot thank you enough for what you did for us outside the walls. If you had not spoken up, I shudder to think where we would be now. We would have had to go back north looking for an unlikely bastion to defend," I spoke passionately.

"Oh Marcus, I know how to pull the old heartstrings, even in old goats like De'Beresford. Maybe it's something I learned from Elaine." Vincent paused for a moment at his own mention of his beloved sister's name, before continuing, "Marcus, I came up here to summon you to a council meeting in the chamberlain's office. Please, follow me if you will."

It felt something of a relief to finally have a meeting aboveground and in a secure location, at least for the present. Around the long table sat Lord Harbrandt, Captain Winters, Major De'Beresford, his attendant Captain Eaves, and myself. This was my first time seeing De'Beresford up close. He was a stout soldier in his early 50s, with a large working man's hands and several scars that told of battlefield experience.

He regarded the newcomers with steely blue eyes, before opening the meeting: "Gentlemen, I apologise for turning you away at first. We were under orders to allow no access to those we could not identify, even if they appeared to be fellow Halians. I can imagine that you have trod a difficult path to get here, and in time I may come to hear of it. However, this meeting has been called to discuss the present and the future. It is no secret that the Utreshian forces are amassing on the northern shore of River Sovern and will breach it in no small time. Once they have means to transport troops across the water, we are the only thing standing between them and Farchester."

I felt encouraged that De'Beresford had no intention of abandoning Mirgot's Pass and seemed to take his duties seriously.

"I feel that trying to confront them as soon as they step off their makeshift bridges is folly, although such an idea has been raised. We may cut down a few, but the sheer weight of them driving into us would be a massacre, OUR massacre. I say we man these walls and do everything we can to break them here," continued De'Beresford.

There were nods and murmurs of assent at the table. I didn't believe any of us thought that rushing out in a final blaze of glory was a good idea, given our depleted numbers. Better to plant ourselves behind the protection of large stone walls built for the very purpose of keeping Halia safe.

"I would agree with that plan, Major. How many soldiers in total are within Mirgot's Pass now?" enquired Captain Winters.

"With your reinforcements, I reckon we have maybe forty fighting men at hand. Most of your soldiers arrived with their own weapons and armour. We also have a fairly stocked larder, so won't starve anytime soon," came the Major's response.

"Is there any chance of reinforcements from Farchester?" Lord Harbrandt asked.

"Sadly not, my Lord Harbrandt. Farchester is in a precarious state. They already have the majority of their fighting forces campaign abroad. The outbreak of Devil's Curse is still rife in the streets, and this has brought its own disturbances as the commoners protest and even riot in the streets for better living conditions. Essentially, they have their hands full. They need all the soldiers they have just to keep order," the Major informed us.

There was a morbid silence as the meeting attendees digested these facts, until the silence was interrupted by a knock at the door. Upon being invited in, the caller nodded respectfully and briskly delivered the following message: "Pardon me for interrupting, Major De'Beresford, but there is a matter of urgency. An Utreshian peace delegate has arrived. They say that they have no affiliation with those attacking our lands. They wish a parley. They are currently still outside."

The Major thanked the messenger, before standing and drawing the meeting to a close, but not before advising everyone that another meeting would not be far away. It was understandable that the Major would be eager to speak with this Utreshian party. Frankly, any information or conversation would be of use. Other than the brief display of guarded civility Va'heash and his dogs had displayed at Carnagon Castle, the only thing we had seen from them was bloodshed and violence.

The Major called Captain Winters and I to his side in the narrow corridor outside the chamberlain's office. "I would ask you two to attend this meeting with me. After speaking with some of your lords, I understand that you, Captain Kane, managed to escape from Carnagon Castle after it was sacked by the invaders. Captain Winters, I heard that you were able to lead a group of soldiers away from Barford Castle after being overwhelmed by a vicious attack. I cannot imagine what you have been through, but you have direct experience and knowledge which may be useful in this meeting."

Both Kurt and I agreed to attend the meeting. I took the opportunity to ask the Major if Lord Harbrandt should attend. The Major pondered this question, looking thoughtfully at the floor and rubbing his grizzled chin.

"Mmm...I have heard something of Lord Harbrandt's harrowing experience at Carnagon; I cannot even imagine what he must have gone though. Very well, if you feel he would be of use then by all means go and speak with him, but I would rather we dealt with this issue as soon as possible, so be quick about it please."

I acted on this instruction and wasted no time in tracking down and speaking with Vincent. I found him as he was descending the stone steps to one of the larger halls. After a brief discussion, Vincent agreed to attend the meeting alongside De'Beresford, Kurt and I.

It was a mere five minutes later that the four of us walked back out of the same solid door through which we had entered not long ago. Major De'Beresford took the lead, as we slowly approached the Utreshian party waiting patiently for us some thirty feet outside the fortress walls. There were three of them, apparently unarmed and carefully guarded by four Halian foot-soldiers all carrying 6-foot spears.

My concern about the presence of weapons was clarified by the lead guard, "We checked them carefully for weapons, Major. They are unarmed."

"Thank you, Lieutenant Jones, please could you give us a moment with our guests? Just stay close by," ordered the Major.

Lieutenant Jones nodded before leading his guard away from what was about to be the first Halian-Utreshian peace conference of this war. In truth, I know that we all felt a buzz of excitement.

The Major spoke first, "I am told that you are not a part of the same army savaging our once beautiful lands. So, who are you and what do you want?" demanded the Major in a stern tone.

One of the Utreshians, a tall man with tanned skin and a very stern-looking face, stepped forward a pace, as if to indicate that he would be the lead negotiator. He wore a knee-length brown robe belted at the waist, with thick cotton trousers and sturdy leather boots. His long jet-black hair was worn long and tied in a ponytail.

"I am Ravaise, a warrior from South Utresh. I travelled here with whatever men I could find upon hearing about what the Utreshians from the north had started here. You see, we share the same enemy. We have been feuding with these…monsters…for years now. I can explain further, if you will allow, but what we want is to aid you. To help you defeat the Purgorites and reclaim your land," came the opening statement from what we could now call the South Utreshian party.

"Purgorites? I have not heard that name before. What do you know of these beings?" asked the Major.

"*Purgorites* is the name of their cursed clan. They are ruthless invaders and barbarians, who employ all manner of savagery and brutality in securing their conquests. They are truly dark and twisted. No remorse, no compassion, no mercy. They can move from land to land like a plague, taking over and ravaging the place before moving on," Ravaise responded.

"Yes, several of us have had a taste of their brutality. We have seen what they are and had a taste of the evil they are capable of," interjected Vincent Harbrandt.

I took this opportunity to ask Ravaise about the mysterious Lord Va'heash and his enormous champion. His response made me wish I hadn't asked.

"Lord Va'heash is essentially the overlord of the Purgorites. He is cunning and silver-tongued, using guile and deception to progress his desires. He is a master of manipulation, and many fear he possesses dark powers of mind control. This unnatural discolouration of the sky is Va'heash's doing, I am almost certain. Purgorites of his level learn the ability to alter even elements of the weather itself, like rain, cloud, air quality."

"You see, North Utreshians cannot operate under the sun of many foreign lands, so to operate during daylight hours, they must provide a cover to protect themselves. This sickly-looking sky above us is basically protection for them. Unfortunately, as I have seen before, the plants, trees and crops wither on the ground. As for the huge beast that tends to travel in Va'heash's shadow, that creature is called Brutuck, although he has been known by other names. He is a walking nightmare; a strength and ferocity I have not seen come from a single being before. I fought against him once, and his destruction was shocking to witness."

"I watched in horror as he waded into a solid pack of some twenty troops, hacking and slashing into them like a plough going through corn. His eyes seemed to be on fire during this onslaught, as blood flew in all directions. The men he was fighting didn't stand a chance, even with their armour and weaponry. He, or 'it', was screaming like something not of this world. In a rage, Brutuck is truly unstoppable. You would be wise to keep those high walls between you and him," Ravaise informed our group.

"We would be unwise to turn away help at such a time, it is true," opined Major De'Beresford, before asking Ravaise a direct question, "Ravaise, say we accepted your offer of assistance, how many soldiers could you bring to our aid?"

"I have a hundred soldiers prepared and camped not far from here. A small force, I know, but they are seasoned warriors who will gladly fight to the death against Purgorite scum. I say again, each and every one will fight until they drop."

"I can ask for little more, Ravaise. Very well, I accept your offer of aid. I ask that you remain in your camp for now. I have little doubt that you will see the Purgorites approaching and know when to mobilise yourselves. Please tell me, how do we contact you going forward?"

At this point, Ravaise turned to look at one of his comrades, a similarly attired Utreshian who looked as if he had seen plenty of combat and had no problem seeing more. This man reached into his robes slowly with one powerful-looking hand, as if to let us know that he was not reaching for anything dangerous, before producing a brightly coloured flag. This flag was handed over to Ravaise, who then gifted it to Major De'Beresford, with the following explanation:

"Please, wave this flag from your highest tower. Two strokes if you wish a further parley, and three strokes should you wish immediate military support. We will have eyes on that tower day and night. Do not worry, my soldiers have very sharp eyes. Even at night, we will be able to see the flag moving."

"Very well. Thank you. We will send you the appropriate flag signals as and when. Be ready," spoke the Major.

With those words, the first peace treaty of the war had concluded. Ravaise bowed his head, before turning and moving back into the cover of the nearby woods accompanied by his two comrades.

The four of us watched in silence as Ravaise and company moved out of sight. It was Captain Winters who broke the silence with a good question, maybe THE question: "Do you feel we can trust them?"

"We would be fools to trust foreigners, just because they claim that we share an enemy. We have only just met and have only a few minutes of conversation to go off in terms of forming an opinion. I don't know, this could all be a ruse. All these Utreshians could be on the same team and just trying to trick us. But we have little to lose by accepting their aid. If they do turn against us, well…I figure we'll just be meeting our ancestors a little sooner than planned. Let us go back inside the fortress," came the Major's words.

It was the next day, and only one day before the first wave of vicious attacks against our walls, that Kurt and I came across Sir Henry D'Arten. The man we were supposed to kill as part of Kurt's pact with the Mooden-thing. We were introduced to him in the main hall by Lord Hartwright, who had not been witness to Kurt's recounting of his ordeal with Mooden, so had no idea of Kurt's instructions.

Obviously, Kurt and I acted as naturally as we could. We were polite, interested and respectful towards D'Arten. I can imagine that Kurt did not even dare to mention their possible blood linkage.

I did, however, ask D'Arten if he planned on fighting directly when the Utreshians decided to attack Mirgot's walls. By this stage, there was no 'if' on the table. The Utreshians had huge forces amassed just north of the river, camped and alert. The makeshift bridges looked almost ready to come across. We ourselves had not been sitting idly, though. We had been putting every fighting man through weapon drills, deepening the trenches outside of the walls and driving wicked-looking wooden spikes into the ground, to give the enemy a little more to worry about before they reached the walls. Additionally, piles of stones had been collected and piled next to the few working catapults on the high walls. Anything spare that could fly down through the air and cause an ascending Utreshian attacker some pain had also been moved to the high ground.

D'Arten responded by telling us that he planned to be on the wall and not hiding away when it happened, although he could not tell exactly what role he would take as he had not been a warrior for many years. This was not hard to believe; D'Arten was overweight and generally looked soft. His red face and jowls spoke of a love of rich food and fine wine.

Whilst neither of us disliked D'Arten or even wished his death, Kurt had every intention of following through with the deal when the moment came. The right moment. It was Kurt who had to be holding the blade. It was Kurt who had to draw the blood and make the kill.

I awoke early on the morning of the first attack. I felt a sense of dread as soon as I gained full consciousness and could tell that I wasn't alone. Rather than try and force sleep that wouldn't come, I rose from my cot in the barracks section and dressed myself. My next step was to ascend to the ramparts to see if my fears were justified. As I cast my eyes north, I could see that my fear actually had basis. The Utreshian forces had crossed the River Sovern during the night and now populated the south bank in huge numbers. Even from this distance, I could see that they had drawn their own defence lines and had armed guards patrolling along the makeshift wall of sandbags, spikes and overturned carts.

Preventing the Utreshians from fording the river had never really been our plan as we lacked the resources to hamper them. It was only going to be a matter of time, and that time had come.

Mirgot's Pass was a hive of activity that morning as people readied themselves in different ways; soldiers could be seen checking their armour and weaponry, meetings were held, holy officials heard confessions from those men who did not want to meet their Gods as guilty men, blessings were handed out, engineers did final checks on catapults, crossbows and any other weapon with moving parts that was to be employed in the upcoming battle.

As the day neared high noon, the first ranks of the Utreshians were less than one mile from the wall, a distance that could be covered in a 4-minute run. By now, most of the Halian soldiers had taken their places and were as ready as they could be. They were not all stationed on the high ramparts. Several were stationed at windows, ready to pepper the enemy with crossbow shots. There was also a force gathered by the outer door, ready and in some cases eager to sally out and attack the enemy as and when a good opportunity arose.

A hand-picked soldier had been handed Ravaise's special flag, and stood holding it at the required location, ready to wave the flag when he was ordered to. I stood only around twenty feet from the flag-bearer, trying to control my nerves. Even after countless battles both at home and abroad, this battle was inspiring a special kind of fear in me. I had experienced a small taste of what these creatures could do and was about to get a full meal. I had donned a knee-length chainmail coat, belted at the waist. I had chosen a strong steel helmet with a noseguard to protect my head from any swinging enemy cleavers, and steel bracers and greaves protected my forearms and lower legs respectively. I wielded a good longsword and large wooden shield, which I only hoped would stand up to whatever damage the enemy would throw at me.

Young Simon Fester stood directly to my right. I could think of few better men to guard me from that side. Simon, like many others, was feeling the fear, but he was putting on a brave face and trying to focus on his breathing. The hammer-wielding hero Mordak stood to my left, a huge comforting presence I had to admit. He had managed to locate a fearsome-looking bear's head helmet to grace his large skull. He had adapted his hammer further during our stay. It now looked almost too heavy for a normal man to wield and appeared so fearsome that just looking at it would give the enemy pause!

Beyond Mordak's broad shoulders, I could see Lord Vincent Harbrandt. By now, Vincent looked all of his former lordly self, if not stronger. He wore armour similar to mine and also wielded a sword and wooden shield. His chin was up, his shoulders back, his face set. He had a score to settle with these Utreshian scum, a dead sister to avenge.

I was observing the regal form of Vincent when a fully attired Kurt Winters appeared in front of us. He surveyed the waiting men, looking many of us in the eye, before delivering the best speech I can recall hearing in a very long time.

"Men of Halia, my brothers. There will be no parley, no deals with the enemy. They cannot be dealt with. They cannot be reasoned with. Every man standing here ready for battle has displayed courage and bravery which many would shirk from, and for that I thank each and every one of you. You can all see the enemy, barely one mile away. They mean to take Farchester, to charge into our beautiful Golden City and sack the place. But to do that, they need to get past US! That, my friends, will not happen. We will defend these walls to the last man, if need be, for I can think of no greater honour than to give your life in defence of your country. Look at this foul sky the enemy have brought with them."

At this point, countless sets of eyes raised to the heavens, to look at the sickly-looking cloud cover.

"Men of Halia, we will see the sun again. We will see the plants grow again and the water flow free and fresh. We will see our towns, villages and castles rebuilt stronger and more glorious than ever. We will laugh again. We will be strong and proud again. That all starts now, for we need to stand shoulder to shoulder and send these invading scum back to whatever pit they came from. Stand with me now, my friends. For Halia rises!"

With this final line, Kurt thrust his longsword into the sky, and I swear, I could almost see the sword glimmer and shine, although no sunlight reached it. This triumphant sword thrust was accompanied by an ear-shattering Halian roar that must have been heard for miles around.

The enemy did not let our roar go unchallenged however, for they answered with their own bloodcurdling scream of battle. As the front line of Utreshians started moving forward before breaking into a jog, we prepared ourselves for the fight of our lives.

The Utreshians were not foolish enough to simply charge across the open ground, thus exposing themselves to our projectiles. As soon as they were within arrow-shooting range, the front few ranks hid behind large, thick-looking shields protected with some kind of animal hide. Of course, the archers were ordered to lose a volley down into the throng, and whilst some well-placed or lucky arrows did hit home and drop a few enemies, most stuck harmlessly into the raised shields of the enemy.

The Utreshians had by this stage seen the various obstacles they would need to negotiate before reaching the wall; the sharpened spikes and the deep ditches, which would make any vehicles hard to manoeuvre. The Utreshian front ranks moved cautiously between the spikes, all the while ensuring that they were protected by their shields. The rest of the forces hung back slightly whilst their vanguard attempted to decommission our defences.

Once the vanguard were past the spikes, they adopted a method whereby one soldier worked on sawing through the wood with large saws and their comrades protected their backs with the shields. The archers on the wall had been ordered to choose their targets carefully and loose if they saw an opening, but not to waste arrows needlessly. The catapults were put to work, hurling rocks up and down into the enemy ranks. Fortunately, the aim of the catapult operator was keen, and rock after rock smashed into Utreshians working down below. We could hear the frantic screams even from our place on the wall as another Utreshian was mangled or, hopefully, killed. Any joy or sense of success was short-lived though, as any downed Utreshians were quickly replaced by an eager and fresh soldier from the seemingly endless supply waiting just out of projectile range.

The Utreshians had sawed down the stakes to harmless stubs within 20 minutes, meaning that the first obstacle was already negotiated. The Utreshians were already freakishly strong, and combined with the demonic speed at which they were sawing, what might have taken painful hours for a Halian man took a fraction of the time for these creatures. The ditches, recently enlarged by the strong hands of Halian workers, were 8 feet deep and 5 feet across. This feature presented all too little challenge to the invaders, as they simply lay sturdy 6-foot planks across the ditches at very regular intervals, before making their way across.

It was not long before dozens of Utreshians were moving directly to the wall in close formation, shields now held directly above their heads, as if replicating the armoured shell of a tortoise or turtle.

Our troops had begun hurling rocks directly down onto this armoured formation, but sadly had little effect and were just not heavy or moving at enough speed to break the armour. If a rock did knock a shield askew, then it was righted all too soon. It was then that I saw a sight which chilled my blood.

Others had seen what the enemy was bringing forward through the ranks and called it out loudly, as if to ensure that no one was seeing things.

"Ladders, look at the size of those things. How did they make them so long?"

It was truly an impressive feat of engineering, and even at that moment, I had to give them credit. The Utreshians were bringing forward the longest and sturdiest ladders I had ever seen. Ten or so of these super-ladders were being carried flat on the shoulders of the enemy, but when erected and vertical, I had little doubt that they would be tall enough for any climber to be able to set foot on the wall.

Our sharp arrows and flying rocks continued to fell Utreshians in decent numbers; however, as each one fell, two more seemed to take his place. Unlike our resources, the Utreshians were not limited. There were thousands of them committed to this battle, against our force of maybe forty. Just looking at the pulsating sea of enemies thirsty for our blood was enough to make any warrior tremble, not only that but the animalistic sounds of their roars and shouts.

There was a deafening roar from the enemy as the foot of the first ladder was planted in the ground, around twenty feet from the fortress walls. The other ladders quickly followed suit. Then, we could only watch in horror as the ten ladders slowly but all so surely began rising through the air, the tops of the ladders moving closer and closer to our ramparts. It felt like a nightmare that I was powerless to stop. It became all too real though as I heard the bang of the heavy ladder hitting the top of our ramparts. I saw the top rung of the ladder just inches above the parapet and knew that unless we acted, enemy soldier after enemy soldier was going to be jumping off that final rung to slaughter us.

"Get those ladders off the wall, men. Don't let them climb!" I yelled as I rushed forward to lead by example. I was a captain and leader, and despite my fear, I forced myself to act like one.

I started pushing frantically against the ladder, trying to drive it back out into the air where I hoped it would simply overbalance and fall back down. Another strong soldier immediately joined me, and together, we gave everything we had. I could feel acid burning my muscles. My breath was hot and heavy in my throat. Eyes slitted and teeth barred in a snarl, I pushed and pushed. The weight was enormous though, and I could feel the ladder winning this war of gravity.

I looked down quickly and saw that the first of the monstrous enemies was already a third of the way up, and more of his comrades were ascending quickly just below him. It seemed the Utreshians just wanted to make the ladder as heavy as possible. I looked left and right along the walls and saw with a heavy heart that my fellow Halians were encountering much the same difficulty. Soon, the defending soldiers abandoned their fruitless struggles and focused on the fast-ascending attackers already scaling the ladders. Rock after rock was hurled at the leading assaulter on a ladder, and whilst some of these shots were lucky and sent a hapless Utreshian tumbling from the ladder into the boiling mass of enemies below, the next climber just took his place in moments. The lead climber was now only a few feet from the ramparts, eyes ablaze with rage and hungry for blood.

"Prepare to repel invaders. Don't let them off the ladders," bellowed Captain Winters, sword in hand.

We were successful in cutting down those first climbers of each ladder. I beheaded my enemy as soon as he showed his ugly face above the ladder and managed to split the skull of the next climber. Trusty Mordak exploded a few skulls with his legendary hammer. However, we simply lacked the manpower to repel invaders from all ten ladders, and despite the numerous enemies we dispatched, it was only a matter of time before the first Utreshian feet touched down on the ramparts of Mirgot's Pass. So that was it, the enemy was now on the walls.

Whilst I was distracted momentarily by the bold Utreshian who had just alighted upon the rampart, the next climber on the ladder I was dealing with aimed a vicious cleaver blow at my head. I managed to react just in time and parry the strike, but the Utreshian immediately recovered from my manoeuvre, as if expecting it, and swung his free fist in a huge arc. His large, armoured fist exploded against my jaw, knocking me back a few paces, which of course gave him adequate time to jump off the ladder and join the growing number of his comrades on the ramparts.

I righted myself and cut down this challenger without too much trouble but saw that the next climber was right behind. He opened the throat of the Halian soldier who had been fruitlessly trying to help me push the ladder away from the walls moments ago, before turning his wrath on me. We exchanged several lethal blows, my arms already tiring with each block and strike as I had had no time to rest. Time to rest was not a luxury any of us could afford. I gritted my teeth, dug deep within me, and kept fighting.

By this stage, the assigned flag waver had already given the signal to the South Utreshians, and we were just praying that they would come to our aid. I did a quick check of our situation on the ramparts. Whilst several Halian soldiers lay dead and bloodied on the stone floor, I took relief in seeing Mordak, Kurt, Simon, Vincent and Gustav still standing and battling valiantly against the foe. The wall still held, for now, but more Utreshians were launching themselves from the ladders, ready to wade into the melee and send anyone wearing a Halian uniform into the next life. We could not hold the wall for much longer.

I heard a new roar from below and ran to the very edge of the battlements to look down. It did not take long to see that our calls for aid had been answered.

"It's Ravaise, he's come to help us!" I yelled out to my comrades, hoping that this knowledge would aid their strength and give them fortitude when it was needed most.

I looked back down quickly, to see Ravaise lead an army of some three hundred soldiers into the side of the North Utreshians far below. His original given number of one hundred had either been a trick, or he had managed to draw more southerners to his banner. I could not watch Ravaise's progress for long, as I had my own battle to fight, but he seemed to be doing some serious damage. His front ranks seemed to roll right over the siegers closest to him. I wished Ravaise luck, before rushing back to help my brethren. I saw that only three of the ten enemy ladders still had Halian soldiers managing to repel the attackers before they alighted upon the battlements.

Kurt, Mordak and Simon were fighting shoulder to shoulder, against a seven-strong pack of furious Utreshian warriors, and I could see that they were losing. I sprinted forward, longsword held aloft, before slicing down deeply into the exposed neck of the nearest Utreshian. Simon managed to drop another with a deft sword strike through the heart.

Kurt grabbed me by the arm and looked at me with frantic eyes. Sweat poured down his reddened face. He appeared to have sustained no serious injuries though. "Where is D'Arten? We need to do the ritual NOW, or we will lose this wall!" yelled Kurt, having to make himself heard over the screams, grunt and clashes of battle.

I looked around desperately, scanning the faces of the soldiers still standing, to see if I could spot the face of D'Arten. I could not see him anywhere and feared that his comment about standing on the wall and not hiding away was bravado. I was about to ask Kurt if he could hold the wall whilst I ran to demand reinforcements, when I heard yells from behind me.

Kurt and I turned our heads to see several Halian soldiers emerging from the top of the steps which led from the lower areas to the battlements. Praise be, I spotted D'Arten amongst the newly arrived unit, running with a spear in his hands. In that moment, I almost wanted to tell Kurt not to go through with it, that we would be murdering a fellow Halian in cold blood. However, it was not my decision. It was Kurt who had made a deal with a demon. A deal which we had to just hope would save us, somehow.

"You need to do it now, Kurt. You need to kill D'Arten now, or we will lose this wall and likely this whole battle!" The words actually spilled from my mouth.

Kurt looked harrowed but nodded in acknowledgement. There were over 25 Utreshians on the battlements by this stage. The Halian defenders still standing numbered maybe ten and were getting driven back. Many Halian corpses littered the stone flags. I watched in dumb horror as the mighty Mordak was felled by an enemy blade—a vicious strike that took off his whole right arm at the shoulder. My brave and good friend dropped to the ground, before being finished off by the angry Utreshian mob. Later on, I would reflect that Mordak died the only way he knew how—in battle.

Kurt approached D'Arten hastily and uttered only one word, 'sorry', before he slashed horizontally at D'Arten's neck, cutting deep into his jugular and dropping the mortally wounded man whom he barely knew to the ground. His own half-brother. D'Arten spluttered shockingly as his life liquid jetted out of his neck wound.

For Kurt and I, time basically stopped, as we waited, as we hoped, for something to happen. Kurt had fulfilled his part of the deal. Would the Mooden-thing fulfil his?

The first thing I felt was a shift in the air, in the very atmosphere. Then, I saw that above the still corpse of D'Arten, some manner of dark portal was materialising. The portal grew wider and seemed to hum and shudder with a malign presence. The battle seemed to stop, as I saw that the portal appeared to lead somewhere, although my mind could never grasp where that was. I did grasp though that something was coming through the portal, into this realm. I felt every hair on my body rise. I felt my pulse quicken even further. I felt like my eyes were bulging out of their sockets. I could only watch in awe, and I knew that I wasn't alone. I could sense men watching all around me, both Halian and Utreshian.

A figure, which seemed to be made of shadow and darkness itself, dropped from the portal and landed with a thump on the stone flags, as if signifying its reality in our world. The shadow-being then stood, or I should say, *towered*. Red eyes glared menacingly from a skull-shaped head. The shadow-being then raised two long wicked-looking spikes, one in each arm, which seemed to be made of roiling black smoke.

The shadow-being almost seemed to nod at Kurt Winters, as if thanking him, before descending on the Utreshian invaders like an angel of death. The fatigued and baffled Halian soldiers watched with jaws agape as the shadow-being tore and ripped into the Utreshians on the wall. They could not stand against it. Utreshians were viciously hacked in two, sent flying from the wall, beheaded on the spot, disembowelled or just plain mauled by the unstoppable being of smoke, shadow and dark energy.

The dreadful shadow-being, having massacred the invaders on the battlements, then descended with a screech into the huge mass of enemies below. Any Halian soldier still standing rushed to the edge of the wall and looked down. I was gladdened to see that the South Utreshians were still holding firm, and despite numbering less than their original three hundred, were still fighting on, huge piles of North Utreshian corpses at their feet. I swear I could see brave Ravaise himself, felling enemy after enemy like some whirlwind of death. If he lived, I knew that I could never repay him for his courage.

Our attention was then shifted to a new threat. Whilst we had been looking down at the progress of the shadow-being and the South Utreshians, a new figure had joined us on the battlements. I felt my heart stop in my chest as I observed the monster Brutuck only twenty feet away. It seemed that he had chosen his moment carefully and climbed the wall alone, away from the other ladders.

Brutuck was truly a fearsome sight, a giant clad almost head to toe in heavy armour and wielding an absurdly large sword. He grinned savagely at our meagre party from under a metal helmet shaped like a rhino head. His eyes shone yellow and feral. There was no shadow-being on the wall any longer to help us. It was Brutuck against us. I readied myself, sword held in a defensive stance. Kurt stood to my right, blade ready. Simon stood directly to my left, also ready for combat. The few other brave soldiers fell in around us to form a small wall of Halian steel. We had all come so far and gone through so much, it was time to end this. Once more, I heard my father's voice, almost as if he was standing right there on the wall with us: "Rise, Marcus, and don't look back."

The monster Brutuck began slowly walking forward, his blade held out in front of him. The sword Brutuck carried must have been six foot long and looked to weigh upwards of 50lbs. I tried not to think of what he could do with that sword, but what I could do with mine. He could smell our fear and seemed to be enjoying it, savouring it. This was clearly a being who enjoyed invoking the terror that he did. Yes, there was fear in us, but there were other things which I would like to think were helping to drive the fear back. Hope. Courage. Faith.

Brutuck grinned evilly as his yellow eyes fell upon and recognised Vincent.

"Oh, it's you, the feeble little lord who let us just walk into your supposed castle. Your sister did at least…entertain us…for a while. How she screamed. How they ALL screamed! Ha ha ha!" mocked Brutuck in his guttural tones.

I turned to warn Vincent not to cave in to the monster's taunts and keep his head but could see that he was barely keeping his emotions in check. The look of hatred and rage on his face shocked even me, despite all we had been through. His eyes blazed and every muscle in his face seemed ready to snap. Vincent was clenching his fists something fierce, but I noticed that his right fist was wrapped around something. Without any warning, Vincent raised and cocked his right arm, before unleashing whatever he had been holding directly at the laughing head of Brutuck.

As the object sailed through the air, as if in slow motion, I noticed that it was an apple-sized rock. Vincent's throw was true. The rock flew hard and fast and found its home. Brutuck roared in surprise and pain as the rock hit his right eye socket. It was clear that even the mightiest animal can be caught off-guard, and that was exactly what Brutuck was—just another animal. He could be hurt; he could be killed.

"Strike now, men!" Kurt yelled to his battle brethren, seeing the opening.

And so, we all rushed forward to whatever fate awaited us. Brutuck recovered all too early though and swung his vicious blade at our party. Whilst I and several others managed to duck or swerve at the last moment, I heard a sickening sound of metal hitting flesh and felt a torrent of hot blood wash over the back of my neck. Even in that instant, I hoped that the dead Halian was not someone close to me, not Kurt, Simon, Vincent or Gustav. Gods forgive me.

I had no time to look about me though, for I was almost toe-to-toe with the furious giant. I launched into a vicious upward strike with my longsword, aiming for one of the few exposed parts of Brutuck's body. Brutuck was instinctive enough to jerk his head back at the last moment, thus allowing my blade to sail into thin air. Brutuck then grabbed me about my neck using his spade-like left hand, still holding his enormous sword in his right hand. Almost immediately, I could feel the immense pressure he was applying and knew that within precious seconds, everything would go dark.

I felt myself lifted several feet into the air. I looked down on my brethren, who were fighting Brutuck with everything they had. But he kept fending them off and keeping them at bay. He was so much taller than everyone. As my vision darkened and sound seemed to go out of the world, parts of my life flashed before my eyes.

I was running through fields of glowing corn as a happy youth, I was struggling up Redcrag Mountain with my father, I was training in the castle courtyard as a youth, I was campaigning in foreign lands, I was drinking with my friend Vincent in a cosy tavern. Then, just as I felt like I was about to give up and leave this life, I saw the glorious Halian flag. I saw it flying high in a blue sky, a blue Halian sky that I wanted to see again.

Using the last of my strength, from somewhere so deep I doubt I will ever be able to access it again, I swung my legs up so that they were resting on Brutuck's huge shoulder. Then, by enclosing Brutuck's huge left arm with my own body, I managed to twist my body with such force that I dimly heard a vicious snapping sound. I then felt myself fall back to the ground, barely conscious, but I knew that I was not dead yet.

I was helped to my feet by strong Halian hands, and gradually the sights and sounds began to come back into focus. Brutuck was shaking his now broken left arm, as if somehow trying to unbreak it. During everything that had been going on, the nimble Simon Fester had managed to angle behind the monster, and I saw what he was going to do just before he actually did it.

Simon had seen Brutuck's slightly exposed ankle and aimed an expert blow at this exposed part. Brutuck issued another cry of pain as Simon slashed in deep and severed his tendons. Brutuck was by this stage semi-blinded, with a broken arm and one wounded lower leg. But a beast can be at its most dangerous when wounded. I saw Kurt move around to the front of Brutuck, most likely to deliver the killing blow. As much I wanted to see Kurt strike true and end the fight, a deeper part of me knew that it was never going to be that easy.

As Kurt went to drive his longsword into Brutuck's exposed eyes, Brutuck still had a few tricks up his sleeve and was not ready to die yet. As Kurt's longsword flew towards his face, Brutuck quickly picked up a sword from a fallen Halian soldier with a speed none of us were expecting, before knocking aside Kurt's blade and plunging the sword deep into Kurt's chest, easily bypassing the armour he was wearing. Kurt had one final gift for his friends though, for even as his life blood was seeping from his body, he grabbed hold of Brutuck's wrist and held with all his might, thereby trapping Brutuck's only useful hand.

"Now Vincent, the kill's yours. Go for the eyes!" Poor Kurt said with his last few breaths, now spitting blood along with the words.

Vincent Harbrandt did not hesitate. He moved in and grasped one of Brutuck's helmet horns with his left hand and used his right to drive a long dagger into both of Brutuck's eyes, again and again and again. Vincent stabbed until he was grunting with rage, effort and pain. Brutuck's face was a mess. The rest of us watched on, not interfering, just waiting for Vincent to burn out his rage. Vincent did indeed burn out after countless stabs, dropping to his knees and leaning against the wall. Then Vincent's tears came. He sat right by Brutuck's still body, crying helplessly, his face in his hands.

I went to check on my old battle brother, Kurt. He was lying still, his hand clasped over his gory chest wound. His blood had pooled beneath him and he was taking shallow breaths, which I knew were numbered. Our eyes met as I took his hand in mine.

"Halia has risen, Kurt. You fought well, my brother."

Kurt, now basically beyond speaking, offered me what smile he could and nodded slightly. He held out his right hand, fingers spread, as if wanting something. I did not have to ask what he needed. I quickly returned to him with his longsword and placed the handle in his outstretched hand. Kurt wrapped his hand around the handle one last time. He held the sword with both hands flat against his body, hilt just under his chin and tip pointing towards his knees. Kurt then left this life, dying a true soldier of Halia. My own tears would come in time, but I did not weep right then.

It was then that the blaring sounds of horns sounded from far below. Despite our fatigue, the remaining soldiers on the wall stood, looking about to see from whence the sound came. The horns blasted again, and this time my mind was clear enough to tell what they were.

"Those are Halian horns," I confirmed.

We all rushed to the south side of the battlements, as the sounds of the horns were coming from the south, from the direction of Farchester. I looked down, and at first, I thought that I was hallucinating, that all this fear, violence and bloodshed had addled my senses. But then, others called out what they saw.

"It's the Halian army, there's hundreds of them. They took their bloody time!"

Down below, a huge Halian force of cavalry, archers and foot-soldiers was rushing to our rescue, to the very rescue of Halia. I did not have time to count, but I saw several hundred at least. Even though the horrid smog was still infecting the clouds, I could almost see their armour and weapons shining, as I had done Kurt's sword. I found myself roaring approval from the ramparts and raising my bloodied sword into the air. Every man amongst us did the same and took up the cry. We shortly heard the sounds of the main gates slowly opening. We knew what was about to happen, so shifted ourselves to the other side of the battlements to follow the progress of our Halian warriors.

The Halian riders spurred their horses to a canter, before shifting into an all-out charge, roaring glorious war cries of their own. The line of cavalry, seven horses wide, exploded out of the other side of the Mirgot's Pass like a shining battering ram of muscle, steel and rage. Our cavalry smashed mercilessly into the already wounded and weakened mob of Purgorites. The Purgorites, the mighty enemy we had once feared and hid from, were being trampled under hoof, broken, sent flying or beheaded like lambs to the slaughter.

The cavalry charge did not seem to lose momentum, the warriors just kept ploughing deeper into the mass of enemies. Their bloodied swords rose and fell whilst their long razor-sharp lances swept enemies off their feet. The foot-soldiers followed in close behind, not breaking apart, but fighting as a solid wall of steel. They ruthlessly cut down the Purgorites still standing, or even down but not out. No quarter was given. No prisoners were being taken.

I looked to my right and saw that the brave South Utreshians were continuing to give an excellent account of themselves. They had gained solid ground during the battle and ended up fighting only feet away from the Halian foot-soldiers. I only hope that they did not mistake the South Utreshians for our northern enemy; luckily, I did not spot any conflict between the two forces.

After the ranks of foot-soldiers had moved in to back up their mounted brethren, the lines of archers began to form up in disciplined rows of three. Halian archers were trained in the use of the longbow, a professional archer capable of sending an arrow over 1,000 feet. The archers, rather than shoot at nearby targets, instead raised their longbows into the air, before drawing back the strings almost to their chins and releasing as one, on command.

We on the wall watched in awe as wave after wave of deadly arrows flew high into the air, before descending clear over the heads of the cavalry and down into the mob of Purgorites. Whilst some arrows missed, more than enough seemed to find its way into an enemy body as we saw countless enemies fall to the ground. It was not long before the combined assault of the Halian and South Utreshian forces had broken the Purgorites. They began to turn and flee northwards, not as an ordered disciplined retreat, but more of a cowardly and pathetic refusal to fight to the death. The foreigners had come looking for an easy conquest and we had denied it to them.

The Halian cavalry did not accept this retreat however, and those still in the saddle, some two-hundred-strong, chased after the retreating scum like bloodthirsty hounds after rabbits. It struck me that once the Purgorites reached the wide river, they would likely become stuck. I had the strong idea that their arrogance had allowed for no retreat plan. If this was the case, then once they reached the river, the Halian cavalry, and the ranks of foot-soldiers following close behind, would cut them down. I hoped that this would be the outcome; however, soon enough, the battle had moved north, almost out of our field of vision.

"Marcus, my friend."

I turned my head from what was left of the battle to see trusty Brother Abel approach me. He was unharmed and looked whole, although I did not ask exactly what he had been doing in the fight. That talk would come later, hopefully with a pint of brown ale in our hands. We embraced each other warmly, before I spoke: "We have done it; the battle is over. I can see the scum fleeing northwards. What is left will not get far with our riders in hot pursuit."

"I am so glad to see you alive, Marcus, I was at one of the arrows slits on the third floor, hurling everything I could down at the enemy. I saw all those damn ladders get raised and dreaded to think what you brave souls up here would have to face." Brother Abel broke off to look around, before seeing some of the bodies lying still on the ground. "Oh, poor Captain Winters. I don't need to ask if he died bravely. He is a hero, Marcus, you all are."

I nodded at Abel in gratitude, already feeling a lump in my throat and fearing that my voice would betray my emotions if I spoke. Luckily, Abel then looked down at the wretched corpse of Brutuck, his face a mask of disgust.

"So, their champion lies defeated. Not so unstoppable, after all. What should we do with the body, do you think?" asked Abel, looking at me for a response.

"I don't know, mount his wretched head on a pike outside the Farchester gates, cut him up for pig feed, maybe send his body back to…Lord Va'heash," I replied.

Lord Va'heash himself had not occurred to me during the battle. I had not seen him in person since that fateful night at Carnagon Castle. I do not believe he had been directly involved in the battle. I had a horrible feeling that we would be seeing him again, whether we liked it or not, and that the Halian-Utreshian war was far from over.

For now though, Halia had been rescued. The Purgorites' mighty champion lay dead and their army had been soundly broken and beaten at Mirgot's Pass. Halia was safe.

I was about to ask Brother Abel about our next steps, when I detected a presence behind me. I turned, almost knowing what I would see. I was still startled and unnerved at first, but only for a moment. It was the shadow-being which D'Arten's bloodletting had brought into this realm. I stood facing the shadow-being, although if I focused and looked closely, I could almost see Mooden himself within the shadow. I put my arm on Brother Abel's shoulder, as if to assure him not to be afraid.

"Captain Winters fulfilled his part of the bargain. I am sorry that I cannot thank him in person. At least Captain

Winters died in service of his country, sword in hand. There are few better ways for a soldier to die. I have been avenged. I can rest now," spoke the shadow.

Then, for a moment, I saw Teryn Mooden as he had lived as a Halian soldier. Just for an instance, he stood before me, a handsome and smiling fair-haired man, proudly wearing his uniform. He spoke two words, in his own voice, before finally disappearing and moving on to whatever lay ahead of this mortal life: "Thank you."

So ends my story. The Purgorite invaders were defeated that day at Mirgot's Pass, and whilst some stragglers did escape to the coast and flee back to North Utresh, most were hunted down and slain. Praise be, the foul fog which had been hanging over our land for too long cleared, allowing a pure sun to shine on our faces once more. Plants, crops and trees began to grow healthily once more.

I travelled back north after several days of rest at Farchester, as part of a contingent to reestablish a Halian presence at our old base at Carnagon Castle. Young Simon Fester and Brother Abel were by my side, and I could never thank them enough. Rebuilding projects sprang up all over Halia in a bid to repair the damage wrought by the Purgorites. It would be a slow process, but we were together.

Lord Vincent Harbrandt returned to his family seat at Gutvast Palace. He was the never same man after what he had been through, though he was determined to be a more able ruler and never allow another invasion like this to occur again. I still think of the friends and comrades I lost during the war, and whilst they are gone from us, their sacrifice and bravery will never be forgotten. Halia rose, and may it never fall again!